GO

GO

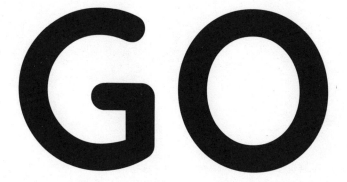

KAZUKI KANESHIRO

TRANSLATED BY TAKAMI NIEDA

Previously published as *GO* by Kodansha in Japan in 2000 and republished by KADOKAWA CORPORATION in Japan in 2007. Translated from Japanese by Takami Nieda. English translation rights arranged with KADOKAWA CORPORATION, Tokyo through Japan Uni Agency Inc., Tokyo. First published in English by AmazonCrossing in 2018.

Published by AmazonCrossing, Seattle
www.apub.com

ISBN-13: 9781503937376 (hardcover)
ISBN-10: 1503937372 (hardcover)
ISBN-13: 9781542046183 (paperback)
ISBN-10: 1542046181 (paperback)

Cover design by David Drummond

Printed in the United States of America

What's in a name?
That which we call a rose
By any other name would smell as sweet.

—Romeo and Juliet

Leah strode back eastward toward Monroe, working up to a trot and then to a run. The orchestra of car horns behind her grew louder, and then, after a minute, the sound was augmented by the distant scream of sirens, which soon overwhelmed the horns, eventually silenced them, and took their place.

Leah had slowed the movement of traffic across the river from Monroe toward West Monroe to a complete stop. She ran hard toward the sound of sirens, hearing them grow louder and louder. Just as she reached the end of the swing bridge, she spotted the Chevrolet Malibu with the four men in it. They had pulled up into the traffic jam, trying to shoulder their way ahead. The traffic had by then grown dense enough that they had come to a complete stop. Now the jam in the right lane looked at least a half mile long, and it was growing.

Leah saw the police cars coming, partly because her vantage on the swing bridge gave her a little extra height. She saw about a half dozen police cars, their lights flashing, stop on the approach to the bridge. Behind the first group of police cars, others stopped at angles to prevent civilian traffic from getting past them into the mess on the bridge.

The police officers in the first set of cars opened their doors and got out, some of them pulling on body armor over their shirts, others lifting the shotguns from their cars, and still others advancing between the cars, carrying only their sidearms.

Leah ducked low and began to make her way across the front ends of the stopped cars toward the Malibu. When a man hung out of his window and yelled something at Leah, she drew her pistol and held it muzzle-upward, took out her ID wallet with her badge in it, and held them up to show him and the other drivers nearby. The noise subsided and she advanced.

The badge and gun and the way Leah moved from car to car, sometimes squatting and other times crouching and running, had convinced the drivers near her that she was a cop. The flashing

1

"Hawaii . . ."

I was fourteen the first time my old man uttered that word in my presence. We were watching some New Year's special where these three gorgeous actresses jetted off to Hawaii and kept shouting, "Beautiful!" "Delicious!" "I'm in heaven!" Up until then, Hawaii was known in our house as the symbol of depraved capitalism.

At the time, my father was fifty-four and held North Korean citizenship. He was what the Japanese call Zainichi Chosenjin (a North Korean resident of Japan) and a Marxist.

First, let's get one thing straight. The story that follows is a love story. *My* love story. And communism—or democratism, pacifism, *otakuism*, vegetarianism, or any other -ism for that matter—has got nothing to do with it. Just so you know.

Anyway, when the old man mentioned Hawaii, my mother (also North Korean) clenched her fist in triumph. She whispered to me later, "Your father didn't stand a chance against the infirmities of old age."

Tokyo was hit by a severe cold snap that winter, and I guess my father's fifty-four-year-old body was really feeling it, judging from the way he kept rubbing his joints and muttering about his arthritis. He was born in the temperate climate of Jeju, an island province of South

Korea, and spent part of his childhood there. By the way, Jeju Island is also the self-proclaimed "Hawaii of the East."

My mother was born and raised in Japan. She was nineteen when my father picked her up at Ameyoko Market in Okachimachi and twenty when she gave birth to me.

Seeing how my father was now teetering, my mother spun around behind him and gave him one last push: "The Berlin Wall crumbled, and the Soviet Union doesn't even exist anymore. Just the other day, the people on TV were talking about how the cold temperatures caused the Soviet Union's fall. The cold freezes people's souls . . . their ideological beliefs, even," she said with a shiver. I half expected her to burst into a mournful song.

My father listened with his body stooped slightly forward as if to keep from toppling over. When he looked up and turned his gaze to the television, the three actresses, now wearing bathing suits, turned their rapt faces toward him and called out, "Aloha!"

"Aloha," my father muttered.

It sounded like a death moan. My old man let out a long, deep sigh and fell . . . to temptation.

Once my father got up off the floor, he acted quickly. As soon as the holidays were over, he began the process of changing his citizenship from North Korean to South Korean, so he could visit Hawaii.

I should explain. Why did my father, who was born on the South Korean island of Jeju, have North Korean citizenship? And why did he have to change his citizenship to South Korean just to go to Hawaii? It's a tedious story, so I'll try to keep it short and mix in some humor here and there. But don't hold your breath.

Back when my father was a kid during World War II, he was a Japanese citizen. Why? Long ago, Korea was a Japanese colony. Forced to adopt a Japanese name, Japanese citizenship, and the Japanese language, my father was destined to fight as a soldier in the emperor's army when he grew up. He came to Japan as a kid when his parents were drafted to work in the munitions factories. But when Japan was defeated and the war ended, the government no longer allowed him to remain Japanese. And to add insult to injury, the Japanese government said, "We're done with you. Get the hell out of our country," sending Korean residents into a panic. Before they knew what happened, the United States and the Soviet Union had divided the Korean peninsula into two countries. So Koreans were allowed to stay in Japan but were forced to choose between South and North Korean nationality. My old man chose North Korea because it touted Marxist ideology and was assumed to be more compassionate toward the poor. And because it showed more concern than the South Korean government for Koreans living in Japan. That's how my father became a North Korean resident of Japan.

My aging father, having switched his citizenship twice by a young age, was now attempting to change it a third time. He couldn't get a visa as a North Korean because that country didn't have diplomatic relations with the United States. Since North Korea had so few diplomatic ties with other countries, North Korean residents of Japan were limited in where they could travel. I've heard that you can get a visa for some countries, but with the red tape and hassle, there was no telling how long that could take.

So what my father did was appeal to a Mindan leader. Ready for some more tedious explanation? Here goes . . .

In Japan, there are basically two ethnic Korean organizations: Chongryon and Mindan. Generally, North Korean residents of Japan associate with Chongryon and South Korean residents with Mindan. Reflecting the relationship between North and South Korea, and like the feuding Montagues and Capulets, the two groups clash every now and then but maintain a reasonable distance from one another. You know how *Romeo and Juliet* ended, right?

Long ago, my father had been an active member of Chongryon. He spent all his free time fighting for the rights of fellow North Koreans living in Japan and donated tons—I mean *tons*—of money to "the sound management of the organization." But all of his efforts and years of service went unrewarded. I really can't go into the details here, but basically, my father realized that Chongryon was more concerned with North Korea than with the North Koreans living in Japan. Around the same time he'd lost hope in North Korea and Chongryon, the temptation of Hawaii had taken hold.

Anyway, the first thing he did to get his South Korean citizenship was talk to someone he knew in the Mindan leadership. This was the same guy who'd asked my father to spy on Chongryon back when he was still involved in their activities. My father refused—so he says.

This guy told my father that all you need to do to obtain citizenship is go to the South Korean embassy, fill out the proper forms, and wait for the application to go through. But the waiting period varies from person to person. In the case of someone who has exhibited "traitorous inclinations" in the past, such as working for Chongryon, and who was a Marxist to boot, who knew how long it would take the application to go through, if at all. No doubt this uncertainty made my father nervous.

Thanks to some backdoor dealing, my father's application sailed through in just two months. That must've been some kind of record for a former Chongryon Marxist. What did my old man do, you ask? Simple. He bought off the guy with a massive—I mean *massive*—amount of money.

And that's how my father masterfully obtained citizenship for a third time. He wasn't the least bit impressed with himself, though. "You can buy citizenship to any country you want," he used to joke on occasion. "Which country will it be?"

◆ ◆ ◆

At this point, he could have taken off for Hawaii, but there was one last thing my father needed to do. He needed to send a truck to his brother in North Korea.

Which brings me to my last bit of this boring explanation, and there's no finding the humor in this one.

My father came to Japan during the war with a brother who was two years younger than he was. This brother—my uncle, that is—returned to North Korea during the repatriation campaign that began in the late 1950s. The campaign essentially touted North Korea as an "earthly paradise," encouraging persecuted North Koreans living in Japan to return to their homeland and forge a life with their compatriots. At the time, most North Koreans had a vague suspicion that nothing good ever came out of anything called a campaign, but thinking it might be better than Japan, where they faced discrimination and poverty, many went back to North Korea anyway. My uncle was among them.

I'll never forget that first letter my uncle addressed to me. He had written in beautifully penned Japanese, "Send as much penicillin and as many Casio digital clocks as you can. Please, I need your help."

After changing his citizenship to South Korean and effectively betraying Chongryon, my father couldn't help but worry about my uncle. My father had never been to North Korea, and now that he had changed his citizenship, there was little chance that he ever would. He would likely never see my uncle again. And neither of them was exactly young anymore.

Once again, my father managed to put together a massive sum of money, this time using it to buy a three-ton truck, which he shipped to North Korea. My uncle had written in one of his letters that if he had had a truck, he might be appointed the head of the local neighborhood association or something. Along with the truck, my father sent a letter, explaining his change of citizenship. We never heard from my uncle again.

Soon after I entered my final year of junior high school, my old man jetted off to Hawaii with my mother (who had also become a South Korean citizen by then).

Aloha!

Now a huge framed photo of a pretty Hawaiian girl in a straw skirt kissing my father on the cheek decorates the foyer of the house. In it, he's wearing a hibiscus lei around his neck, grinning from ear to ear as he flashes the peace sign. With both hands.

Jackass.

And me?

Finally, I can talk about me. This isn't a story about my father or mother, after all. This story is about me.

I didn't go to Hawaii.

Why?

Since I was the child of parents with North Korean citizenship, I automatically became a Zainichi Chosenjin with North Korean citizenship. Like I said, when I was a kid, I thought that Hawaii was the symbol of depraved capitalism. I grew up surrounded by books written by Marx, Lenin, Trotsky, and Che Guevara. I attended a Chongryon-run Korean school, where I was taught that America was the enemy.

Even so, that doesn't mean that I was infected by communist ideology. I didn't give a damn about North Korea, Marx, Chongryon, Korean schools, or America. I was just living with the circumstances that I happened to be born into. And given those screwed-up circumstances, naturally I became a misfit. I mean, how could I have turned out otherwise?

By the time of my parents' Hawaii adventure, I'd developed into a fine misfit. So I rebelled against my father over changing citizenship. It wasn't that I had any hang-ups about it, but I had no intention of giving in so easily.

One spring day, just before the start of my third and final year of junior high school, my old man forced me into the car and started driving. I asked him where he was taking me, but he continued to drive the car in silence, out of Tokyo and toward Kanagawa.

He's going to kill me!

Why such an extreme reaction? My father had been a nationally ranked lightweight boxer and was the type to punch first and ask later. Punk that I was, I'd gotten hauled into the police station a number of times over some mischief that I'd pulled. My father nearly beat me to death three times.

As I racked my brain for a way to jump out of the car, we arrived at our destination. Tsujido Beach in Shonan.

After pulling the car over to the side of the seaside road, he slammed the car door and started walking toward the beach. "Come with me."

Although the image of my father holding my head underwater until I drowned flashed before my eyes for a split second, as I watched his back, I didn't sense any bloodlust. I decided to follow him to see what this was all about.

He trudged ahead of me in the sand, plunked himself down in the middle of the beach, and stared out at the water. I calculated the precise distance that would put me safely out of his reach and took a seat next to him. I deliberately sat on his right. My father was a southpaw.

He gazed at the sun setting over the early-spring ocean, saying nothing. Meanwhile, I was checking out a cute teenager walking a golden retriever. When our eyes met, she gave me a coy smile. Just as I was about to smile back at her, I sensed a murderous rage on my left. I cursed myself for letting down my guard. My father's fist was flying toward my head.

I'm dead!

I felt his knuckles rap lightly against the side of my head.

"Look straight ahead," he said.

Having escaped what I thought was certain death, I turned toward the ocean and stared. Several minutes passed, and after mumbling something about how he should've chosen a prettier spot, my father turned and fixed a hard look on me. I was terrified. His eyes were dead serious. The two-inch scar at the corner of one eye from his boxing days had turned crimson. I was thinking about cracking a smile to lighten the mood when he finally opened his mouth.

"Take a good look at the wide world," he said. "You decide the rest."

That was it. After saying this, he rose to his feet and left me sitting there on the beach.

I didn't hate him for pulling such a cheesy stunt. Though I may have been a misfit, I was also a romantic. That part about the "wide world" really got my heart pumping.

I sat there on the beach and stared ahead. The ocean was wide open and free. As the sunset gave way to moonlight, I ached with the yearning to put my boat in the water and sail to distant countries.

And so, I gave in. Sure, my father's cheesy performance had something to do with it, but that wasn't the only reason. I had grown up trapped in an environment over which I had no control, but now I had been given a choice. North Korea or South Korea? As horribly limited as my options were, the choice was mine to make. I felt as if I was being treated like a human with rights for the first time in my life.

I agreed to change my citizenship to South Korean but refused to go on the trip to Hawaii with my parents. I asked my father if he'd let me use the travel expenses for something else instead.

"For what?" he asked.

"I want to go to a Japanese high school," I answered, looking my father straight in the eyes.

Most students who start their education in Korean schools typically continue on to Korean-sponsored high schools and universities.

"What's gotten into you all of a sudden?"

My citizenship had changed from North Korean to South Korean almost overnight, but nothing about me had changed. Nothing about me *was* changing, and I was bored. With that change in citizenship, I felt like I had any number of choices before me.

"I want to see the wide world," I answered with the same determination.

A conflicted look of joy and worry came over my father's face. "Do what you want."

And that's how I quit being a North Korean resident of Japan, busted out of the tiny confines of Korean school, and dove into the "wide world." That decision, it turned out, came with some . . . challenges.

The great Bruce Springsteen—he sings about the struggles of the working class. I'm Zainichi. I've got my own struggles to sing about.

> *Thought I was born in a righteous land*
> *Been beaten down about as low as you can*
> *You end up trembling at every touch*
> *Like a dog that's been whupped too much*
> *Born in Japan, I was born in Japan*

That's right.
I was born in Japan.

2

The door flew open.

Some kid, a first-year by the looks of him, stood outside the door, his bloodshot eyes searching the classroom. It was only a week into my third year at the Japanese school.

His eyes found mine and locked on. I decided to ignore him and casually gazed at the anthropology book spread out on my desk. He stepped inside.

The lunch bell had just rung, so there were plenty of students still hanging around the classroom. They dug out what loose change they had in their pockets and began placing bets.

The kid walked past the lectern and made for my desk in the back row, slow and deliberate. I closed the book, slipped it into the drawer of my desk, and kept one hand inside the drawer.

The kid stopped, slightly right of center in front of my desk. He loomed over the chair. I raised my eyes and looked up at his face. He was grunting noisily through his nose. The boy looked nervous, pale, like a child before the start of a race. His chapped lips were pulled tight.

Hurry up and hit me already.

If he attacked me now, I didn't stand a chance. In every altercation so far, not one of my challengers had made the first move. Not a single one. And because of this, I had a 23–0 record and was known through-out the school as the reigning badass.

The kid opened his mouth as if to speak. I decided to cut him off. I was sick of hearing all the tired epithets.

"I'll make you famous," I said. Billy the Kid said this when he drew his guns.

The boy said nothing, letting out only a shallow, puzzled sigh. He might as well have had a question mark floating above his head.

I grabbed the palm-sized ashtray hidden inside my desk, and in one swift move, pulled out my hand and sprang to my feet. His eyes clouded with dark terror the instant they seized on the ashtray. He managed to throw up his arms in defense, but I was faster. Like I said, you really ought to get in that first punch.

I swung and smashed the ashtray against the bulge of his left brow—the supraorbital ridge, to be precise—with a little topspin. The skin there was thin and easy to cut. *Gshhh!* Right on the sweet spot.

As the kid staggered back, his left hand went up to his brow. His eyes were out of focus. He was frozen in panic. I could've finished him there, but I waited. I wanted everyone in the gallery to get a good look.

Within seconds, blood was streaming from between his fingers. People usually react to seeing blood in one of two ways: lose the will to fight or pump themselves into a frenzy. I had no idea which way this loser would react and had no intention of risking it. I decided to finish him off.

I drilled him in the soft part of the knee, putting my full weight into the kick. The kid crashed into a couple of desks and went down on his side. After pushing my desk aside to make some room, I kicked him in the stomach, again and again. Not with the tip but with the top of the foot. A toe kick is harder to pull back on and was liable to rupture the internal organs, not to mention it doesn't make a sound. But with the top of the foot, it was easier to pull a kick, and a well-executed kick makes a thwack or whump sound, making it the perfect deterrent to scare away any would-be challengers in the gallery.

I stopped kicking. He was curled up like a newborn baby, trembling. A terrible feeling of sadness came over me. Damn it if this poor kid wasn't somebody's precious child.

After taking a breath, I slid my desk back to its usual spot. I put the ashtray back in the drawer, took out a tiny bottle of adrenaline solution from my bag, and tossed it in the kid's direction. Just a little of the stuff would stop the bleeding. Honestly, this act of pity wasn't going to do me any favors in the future. The students in the gallery were sure to spread rumors that "Sugihara's gotten soft," which would bring all sorts of challengers like this kid out of the woodwork to take me down. But I think I'm in the clear. Today's trifecta of *ashtray*, *blood*, and *kicking* was a pretty good show, so by the time school got out, the story would have blown up into something like *brick*, *head trauma*, and *bawling*. If the story settled there, they'd be too spooked to challenge me until the start of summer break.

Like Malcolm X said, "I don't call it violence when it's self-defense. I call it intelligence."

I hated violence as much as Malcolm did. But sometimes you don't have a choice. If someone strikes you on the right cheek, do you turn the other cheek? Hell no. Some jerks will bypass the cheek and hit you where it hurts. Even when you've done nothing to deserve it.

I stepped past the kid, still trembling where he lay, and headed for the door. The dagger-like stares from the gallery were so sharp, I could feel them against the back of my head. I spotted three one-hundred-yen coins on top of the desk by the door. Around the desk sat three students. I stopped and asked no one in particular, "Who'd you bet on?"

They looked down at once. I slid the coins into my hand and left the classroom. As soon as I left, I realized that this was the first time I'd spoken to them. We've been in the same class for two years.

I went to the cafeteria and bought some milk with one of the coins I'd just procured. Calcium is calming when you're feeling worked up. The cafeteria was pretty packed, but I managed to find an empty seat at a long table. The others at the table quit talking as soon as I sat down. This was nothing new. I punched the straw through the milk box and drank my milk.

Three minutes later, I was the only one sitting at the table. Once I drained the milk box, I made a game of knocking it over and righting it to pass the time. After I stood the milk box upright for about the twentieth time, Kato came and sat down across from me, a stupid grin plastered across his face. "I heard you took a wrench to someone's head."

So the current rumor going around involved a wrench. I shook my head. "It was an ashtray. You remember the ashtray."

Kato narrowed his eyes and stroked the bridge of his too-prominent nose with a loving finger.

Three years earlier, I'd been admitted to this private all-boys Japanese school, which had a rating about as high as the calories in an egg white. But as someone who'd been educated in Korean schools and studied less than a year for the entrance exams, getting in meant as much to me as if I'd been accepted to the University of Tokyo.

One day about two weeks before the start of the term, I was summoned to the high school. I was shown into the office, where the vice principal and the teacher in charge of incoming first-years asked me to "attend school under an alias to avoid any problems." In other words, they wanted me to take a Japanese name and conceal my heritage, because going by my Korean name might get me bullied.

"I take pride in my name passed down to me by my ancestors. Concealing it would be like throwing away my pride. I won't do it."

Actually, those words never left my mouth. I did as I was told. Why? Because ever since I'd announced my intention to go to a Japanese high school, my Korean teachers had really laid into me. One teacher called me an ethnic traitor. A turncoat. I've been called worse, but more about that later.

Branded an ethnic traitor, I decided to thoroughly betray the ethnicity to which I belong. But even though I'd agreed to go by a Japanese name, I had no intention of hiding that I was Korean. Not that I was going to brag about it either.

At least, *I* wasn't going to do it. But just as you might expect from a second-rate school, the teachers were second-rate too, and they listed the name of my junior high school, which includes the words "North Korean," alongside my Japanese name, "Sugihara," in the student register.

The first challenger appeared before me three days after the entrance ceremony. Korean schools have always been seen as these exclusionary karate dojos crawling with thugs. A *full-contact* dojo, no less. Needless to say, that was just a stereotype. Plenty of tenderhearted guys would rather spend the day in a meadow, weaving poppies into necklaces. Then there are the vicious types who would find no greater pleasure than in fighting brown bears over spawning salmon in a raging current. I'd be willing to bet that Japanese schools have their fair share of both, but sadly, the bears in the Korean schools have been fed a bellyful of discrimination. They keep feasting on that salmon, fattening up, growing more savage by the day. That frightening image is planted in the minds of the Japanese and takes root as the reality for all Koreans.

So basically, to the students at my new school, I was a walking dojo signboard with the word "Korean" written across it. As in *dojo yaburi*— the practice of crashing a rival dojo and challenging its members to a match—if they beat me and returned with my signboard, they'd score points with their pals. Stupid, I know. But it made sense to me.

The first challenger turned out to be Kato. Kato was a bona fide badass, whose father was a top lieutenant in a criminal organization. I was pretty fired up, given how it was my first match, and I broke Kato's nose with an ashtray. Though I beat Kato easily enough, I worried about what his father's crew might do to me. Turned out to be a whole lot of worry over nothing. Kato saw his busted-up face as an opportunity to get plastic surgery on his nose, which he never much liked anyway.

After a while, Kato showed up one day with a sheepish smile, rubbing the ridge of his shapely nose, and said, "Thanks a lot."

His father, who also seemed pleased with the result, said, "You gave my kid an upgrade," and took me to dinner at an expensive restaurant in Ginza. Kato's father was missing the pinky finger on his left hand.

Kato was the first friend I made in high school and the only one I could ever call a true friend.

Kato stopped rubbing his nose and said, as if he had just remembered, "Today's my birthday."

"Well, you're not getting anything from me."

"I wasn't expecting it." Kato produced a strip of paper from the pocket of his school uniform and handed it to me. "A ticket to my birthday party."

"A *party*? Who do you think you are?"

"Well, my old man's paying for it, so . . ."

"How much are you selling these things for?" I asked, referring to the ticket.

Kato smirked and said that it was a trade secret. Shoving the ticket in my pocket, I told him that I'd go if I was feeling up to it.

"There's going to be lots of cute girls there," Kato said. "I promise you a good time." He got up from his seat, clicked his tongue, and added, "I almost forgot. My father wanted me to tell you to come by the house some time."

"No, thanks," I answered. "I don't like yakuza. They bully the weak."

Kato made like he was about to cry. "C'mon, don't hate. He's trying to earn a living, like everyone else. Besides, he really likes you. He's always going on about how you're going to be someone someday."

"All right," I answered. "I'll think about it."

A look of relief came over his face. Kato said, "I'll see ya," and turned to leave.

"Tell your old man I said hi."

The yakuza's son turned around, cracked a broad smile, and held up his hand as if to say, *You got it.*

After school.

I didn't have any friends to hang out with, and after getting kicked off the basketball team the year before, I didn't have anywhere else to go but home. I didn't feel like going straight back, so I killed some time at the bookstore, reading anthropology and archaeology books. Eventually, I bought a book and went home.

When I got home and went into the kitchen for some milk, I found my father sitting at the table with his arms crossed, sullen. There was no sign of my mother.

"Again?" I said, alluding to her absence as I cracked open the refrigerator.

"She says she wants to go to Phuket with her friends," my old man said, pouting.

"So let her, for crying out loud."

"You know we've been struggling lately," he spat out.

Until a few years ago, my father ran four prize-exchange booths for several pachinko parlors. But now that number was down to two. The reason goes something like this: One day, the police paid a visit to a pachinko parlor that my father did business with and informed the owner that my father had deep ties with the yakuza, that his profits were fattening the wallets of the syndicate and bankrolling their activities. Then the police added, "If you insist on associating with those types, we're going to have to keep a close eye on you."

The owner knew full well my father had no ties with the yakuza, but knowing what would happen if he defied the state authorities, he had no choice but to obey. And just like that, the owner ended a twenty-year relationship with my father, and a new exchange booth run by an ex-cop opened for business. Running a prize-exchange booth was a pretty profitable business. True to their nickname—"dogs"—the police have a highly developed sense of smell and an amazing ability to sniff out money.

When my father lost two exchange booths back-to-back, my mother cried foul and discrimination and bloody murder and all sorts of other things.

To this, my father said, "We've still got two booths. We had zero in the beginning. We started with nothing. Now, I may not be good at math, but I know two is more than zero." And he flashed a grin.

In his twenty-six bouts as a professional boxer, my father was never knocked down. Not once did his knee touch the mat. That toughness earned him the nickname "Reinforced Concrete." His ring name was "Hideyoshi Sugihara." As in Toyotomi Hideyoshi, the sixteenth-century ruler of Japan. The name was apparently decided by the gym's owner. It was not a popular name among his Zainichi friends.

One look at my father's grin, and my mother's face had softened into a smile. Soon tears trickled out of the corners of her slivered eyes. "Such a shame."

That same mother had apparently gotten into another argument with my father and left the house for the third time this year. Losing the exchange booths and going to Hawaii had made my mother stronger. The Korean character has always been deeply colored by Confucian ideals, and that tradition was passed on to the Zainichi community. Roughly put, Confucianism was about respecting your elders. In our household, that basically translated to "the wife and child are forbidden to oppose the head of the house."

So at meals, my mother always served the old man two more dishes than herself or me. But after my parents came back from Hawaii, that number increased to four.

"What's with all the extra dishes lately?" my father asked one day after dinner, patting his bulging belly.

My mother, who was in the kitchen, cleaning up, chirped, "I was hoping you'd get diabetes."

While my father was reeling from this unexpected counterpunch, my mother came out of the kitchen and plopped down on a chair. Then she grabbed the weekly magazine from the edge of the table and began reading, the magazine propped up so my father and I could get a good look at the headline on the cover: "Monster Wife Laces Abusive Husband's Dinner with Arsenic!" Peeking out from behind the magazine was a smile as wicked as Jack Nicholson's.

And that's how Confucianism met its defeat. Henceforth, we all got an equal number of dishes, and my mother, who'd rarely been allowed to go out, started spending nights out at the movies, karaoke, and the salon with her friends. My mother was still in her thirties.

After bringing the milk carton to my mouth and taking several gulps, I asked my father, "If we're as bad off as you say, then how come you're golfing all the time? You even bought a membership. You're full of crap."

My father had taken up golf after he came back from Hawaii.

"Golf is the shot in the arm I need to keep me going," he offered lamely.

"You don't think housewives need a shot in the arm every now and then?"

"Let me tell you something about women—"

"North Korea, South Korea, China, and every other country steeped in Confucianism are past their glory days," I cut in. "The days of acting all high and mighty just because you're a man or ridiculously old are over."

My father glowered. "You got a few more years' schooling than I did, and now you're going to lecture me?"

He'd only had an elementary school education because of the chaos during and after the war.

I shoved the milk back in the refrigerator and scooted out of the kitchen. As I climbed the stairs, his voice caught me from behind. "What about dinner?"

I yelled back down, "Instant curry!"

As soon as I entered my room, I called my mother on the cordless. She always stayed with a girlfriend who owned a *yakiniku* restaurant. No one answered at the house, so I called the restaurant. My mom picked up the phone. She said something about being busy prepping for the dinner rush and asked, "How is he doing?"

"I'd give him about two weeks."

"Two weeks . . ."

"Don't worry. I'll survive."

"I'm sorry to put you out. Why don't you come to the restaurant for dinner? Everyone here wants to see you."

"Yeah. Soon, I promise."

After I hung up the phone, I got out of my school uniform and stretched out on the bed in my boxers. I heard *putt, putt, putt* from down below. The old man must've started practicing his putting. Whenever he fell in to a funk, he practiced his putting stroke for hours and hours, like some kind of self-imposed discipline training.

Putt, putt, putt, put, putt . . .

The steady noise began to sound like the gloomy patter of raindrops. I was feeling hungry but was in no mood to eat curry that came out of a pouch. I jumped out of bed, reached into the pocket of the school jacket hanging from a hanger, and took out the ticket to Kato's birthday party. I checked the back of the ticket: the party was in Roppongi. Not a neighborhood I particularly liked. Thinking it was better than being stuck in the house, I decided to go out.

I put on a black turtleneck sweater and some blue jeans. I stuck my head into the living room and told my father I'd be home late. He muttered cheerlessly, "Stay out of trouble," without bothering to look up.

Putt, putt, putt, putt, putt . . .

I'd give him a week.

I left the house.

I got off the Yamanote Line at Ebisu, transferred to the Hibiya Line, and arrived in Roppongi. I turned off Roppongi Street at Almond Cafe and walked all the way down Gaien Higashi Street just shy of Toranomon.

The club where Kato's party was being held, Z, stood away from the main street. When I opened the heavy wooden door, a muddle of dance beats, cigarette smoke, the stench of alcohol, and body heat came flooding out of the dim interior. As much as I tried to dodge any of the offensive sensations, it was no use. I took a deep breath, getting my fill of the fresh outside air, and went inside.

Z was a loft-style club. The first floor where you entered was a loft, and the spacious area below was a dance floor. Takeshita, a kid from school who was always hanging with Kato, was stationed by the door, holding a wad of tickets in his hand. He must have been roped into ticket duty. He mugged a look of shock upon seeing me.

"Didn't think you'd show up," said Takeshita.

I gave him a lazy nod and handed him my ticket. A mob of bodies gyrated to a thumping beat on the floor below. I scanned the loft area. Most of the tables were occupied. Tracking my gaze, Takeshita asked, "Want me to clear you a table?"

Dubious, I asked, "Can you?"

Takeshita shrugged. He walked up to a couple sitting at a round bar table and whispered something in their ears. The couple rose reluctantly to their feet and disappeared down the stairs to the dance floor.

Takeshita returned and made an okay sign with his fingers. When I thanked him, a genuine look of surprise came over his face. I guess my reputation around school is that I'm some kind of jerk.

I made my way to the table against the wall and sat down on one of the stools. The couple next to me was tangled in an intense tongue kiss. I got uncomfortable looking at them, so I leaned out over the railing and stared down at the floor below. People were dancing, giving off heat from every pore, at times looking over their shoulders so as not to bump into the dancers nearby. Their movements looked oddly the same.

A kid with a different air about him was coming up the stairs, holding two glasses. It was Kato. "Thanks for coming." He set one of the glasses on the table and sat on a stool. "Iced oolong tea, right?"

"Yeah, thanks." We clinked glasses. "Congratulations on being born," I said, after taking a sip.

Kato let out a sheepish laugh and glanced downward. "Oh, hey—" He stuck a hand in his pocket, took out a tiny matchbox, and set it on the table.

"What's this?" I asked.

"LSD. You're welcome to it if you want," said Kato, smiling and lowering his eyes timidly.

I adored Kato—this awkward kid who had no clue how to make any display of friendship because he was never taught how, and yet he smiled that innocent, bashful smile.

I gently rapped the back of his hand with a fist. "Thanks, but I don't have time to get high. I've got a lot of things going on in my head. Once I get them figured out, we'll get wasted."

Kato peered into my eyes and grinned as if he read something in them. "Or maybe you'd prefer one of these," he said, holding up a pinky finger, the Japanese gesture for a girl.

I laughed and shook my head. "Nah, but I could use a sandwich or some fruit or something." Kato nodded and got up from the stool. "Hey!" I called out toward his back. When he turned around, I tossed the matchbox at him. Kato made a smooth catch and batted both eyes at me in a failed attempt at a wink.

Just as Kato was descending the stairs, the heavy door opened. A lone girl walked through it. From where I sat, I could only see her from the waist up. Her hair was short, like Jean Seberg's in *Breathless*. I loved Jean Seberg in *Breathless*. Her eyes were round and lovely even from a distance, brimming with the same kind of intelligence as Winona Ryder in *The Age of Innocence*. I loved Winona Ryder in *The Age of Innocence*.

My eyes drifted down to her nose, to her mouth, until she gave her head a toss as if to spurn my advances. The girl handed Takeshita a ticket somewhat absentmindedly and scanned the dance floor. I studied every minute change in her expression. A guy with long black hair and an earring dangling from one ear walked up to her. Throw a rock in Shibuya and nine times out of ten, you'd hit someone that was the spitting image of this guy. He was a clone. I sipped my iced oolong tea, a little disappointed to know that this was the one she was looking for.

The clone leaned in and said something to her. The girl shot him a cold, piercing look that ripped out his heart, crumpled it up into a ball, and tossed it aside. Struck dumb, the clone shrugged in shame before slinking back to where he came from. Clearly, she had a special kind of magnetism that drew the gazes of the men around her. I was no exception. I put down my glass.

Abandoning her search of the first floor, the girl looked to the loft. She resumed her search at one end of the C-shaped loft. I was sitting on the other end. Slowly, her intense gaze passed over the tables one by one, as if she were crossing each one off in her head before moving on to the next.

There were quite a few tables in the loft area. She sighed softly, her eyes stopping about two tables away from mine. The light in her eyes seemed to dim a little. She continued to scan the rest of the tables, as if she simply wanted to finish what she started. Then she came to my table.

Her eyes brightened again. She was staring at me, along with everyone else in the club who'd been tracking her gaze to see where it landed. Despite being taken aback, I fell into to my usual habit and glared. I shot her the most vicious look I could.

Oddly, a smile spread across her face. All the faces in the crowd melted into smiles at once. If I'd smiled too and maybe even given her a big hug, I suppose the story would have ended happily ever after, but that didn't happen. I kept on glaring at her. I mean, I didn't have slightest clue who she was.

As the crowd sensed the unlikelihood of this scenario and began to turn its gaze back to our fair heroine, the heroine in question came toward me with a slight bounce in her step. I honestly thought she was a sister of one the jerks I beat down and that she was going to pull out a knife and attack me, yelling, "*This* is for what you did to my brother!"

But the knife never materialized, and instead she came up to my table and hopped on the other stool. When she landed on the cushion, her short, tartan pleated skirt blew up for a second, giving me a glimpse of her thighs and panties. Both white.

With that afterimage still with me, I looked back up into her unflinching eyes. I braced myself, expecting her to unleash that same devastating look she gave to the clone earlier. But I expected wrong.

The girl smiled and looked right and left as if she were chasing a butterfly fluttering overhead. Then she peered into my eyes expectantly, as if to ask, *Well?* When I blinked and answered with a vacant stare, her eyes traced an arc right to left again, only more slowly this time. For an instant, I wondered if she might be a little wrong in the head. *Maybe she really did see a butterfly,* I thought, but quickly reconsidered. She appeared to be the most right-minded girl I'd ever met.

She fixed a stare at me. But the sad truth was I didn't recognize her face, no matter how good a look she gave me. When I continued to look at her quizzically, she dropped her shoulders a little in disappointment. But soon her eyes were lit with mischief again, as she grabbed hold of the edge of the table with both hands and began swiveling her stool back and forth. Just as I opened my mouth to ask her what she was doing, she twisted her body to the right as far as she could and—whee!—uncoiled her hips and let go of the table at the same time.

Despite capturing every little detail from the back of her head, nape, and back, I didn't recognize any part of her. She spun back around to face me, wearing a smile that seemed to say, *Pretty cool, huh?* She stuck out the tip of her tongue. Years ago, I used to have a puppy that slept with her tongue always sticking out of her mouth. The girl reminded me of the puppy just then.

Finally, I asked, "Do I know you?"

Her smile vanished and gave way to a look colored with resignation. But only for a moment. "Have you ever heard of psychometry?" she asked. Her voice was prim and firm.

I thought about it and nodded. Psychometry was a kind of psychic ability to see the future or past by touching someone or something belonging to that person. I only knew this because I liked *The Dead Zone* and had seen the movie several times.

After seeing me nod, she put her hands over the backs of mine resting on the table. Her fingers were slender, delicate, not bony in the knuckles, straight. Her forefingers slid gently over the backs of my hands. Then they stood on end and moved back and forth on my hands.

"I'm reading you right now," she said softly.

I kept quiet and watched her fingers moving. I can't tell you when humans first began to use their hands, but right then, I wanted to thank that first person.

The girl let go of my hands. That mischievous look came into her eyes again. "You play basketball."

"How did you know?" I asked, making no secret of my surprise.

"I told you, it's psychometry."

I stared at her face in silence for a moment and asked, "What else did you learn?"

24

"You've kicked a couple of people."

I took my eyes off her and scanned my surroundings. Most of the crowd had lost interest in the sight of us. I locked eyes with Takeshita by the door. He put on a bugged-out look of surprise. I scanned the room for Kato. I knew he had to be behind the girl's appearance.

As luck would have it, Kato was coming up the stairs with a plate of sandwiches. Upon reaching the top of the staircase, he caught a glimpse of the girl sitting across from me and knitted his brows. When he came around the table and stole a peek at the girl's face, the vertical creases in his forehead faded, and laugh lines appeared around his eyes. After smiling at the girl politely, Kato set the plate of sandwiches before us, bowed ceremoniously like a well-trained waiter, and moved off.

"Someone you know?" the girl asked.

I tried to read her eyes. She didn't seem like she was acting. Kato didn't look like he was trying to put one over on me either. So what the hell was going on?

The only thing I could think of was that she knew someone at my high school and had pumped him for information about me, but her facts were just a bit off from the actual story. Although I *used* to play basketball, I wasn't exactly playing now, and I didn't kick just a couple of people but a whole mess of people. Even if she did have something on me, what reason would she have for going out of her way to tell me about it? Besides, the only thing any of the guys at school would tell her would've been: "Stay away from him."

"What else did you learn?" I asked again.

As an indifferent smile came across her lips, she said, "That's all for today. Do you want to get out of here? This place is so crowded and claustrophobic and loud and boring, don't you think?"

I couldn't help but ask, "Did you read that from me, too?"

A mysterious smile played on her lips. "Let's go."

She hopped off the stool and headed for the door with the same bounce in her step as when she first entered. I don't know whether or not she was just convinced that I'd follow, but she never once looked back to see if I was behind her. She was right. Her magnetism pulled me right off the stool. But the sandwiches on the table were also giving off their own magnetic force, however faint, and were begging to be sucked into my belly. The girl's back was receding into the distance. I gave up on the sandwiches and left the table behind.

As I opened the door to leave, the people on the dance floor below began to sing "Happy Birthday," a few tentative bars that quickly grew into a rousing chorus. I thought about sticking around to the end of the song out of respect for Kato, but one look at the girl standing on her tippy toes, waving both arms at me, and I abandoned all reservation. I shut the door behind me and ran after her.

We decided to walk toward Tokyo Tower. Not down any particular route, but whichever way our mood took us. The tower, lit up against the night sky, made a good marker.

The girl and I walked in silence, but there wasn't any awkwardness between us. Every so often, she would peer into my eyes, which made me crack an embarrassed grin, and she'd playfully ram her shoulder against me, like a hockey player, with all her might. I once saw a video of this bear cub sniffing curiously at a video camera and then slamming right into it. The girl reminded me of that cub. I wanted to know more about her.

After we walked for about half an hour, I decided to break the silence. "So are you in high school?"

The girl nodded and told me the name of a private school. It was a famous prep school. "I just started year three. Are you second year or third?"

She spoke as if she knew me. "I have as well," I answered. "I just started year three."

She frowned, wrinkling her intellectual forehead. "'I have as well'? That doesn't sound like you."

What did she know about me?

When I told her the name of my high school, she arched a brow as if to say, *Yes, I know.*

"That sweater looks good on you," she said out of the blue. "You look like the boy from *The 400 Blows*."

The 400 Blows was one of my favorite movies. She wore a black knit sweater vest over a dark-blue shirt. The sweater had a red-and-white argyle pattern stitched at the breast. The outfit looked really good on her. I tried to come up with a smooth compliment but couldn't find one. Unable to think of anything better, I said, "That outfit suits you, too." She furrowed her brows again.

What, too formal?

She walked off several strides ahead of me. I might've soured her mood. I shut my mouth and chased after her. There was something I desperately wanted to know; I didn't even know her name yet.

Just as I quickened my pace, she stopped. I stopped alongside her. She was looking off to the side. I turned to where she was looking and saw a gated entrance to an elementary school. The girl was contemplating the heavy iron gate that stood about five feet tall. The school ground stretched beyond it, shrouded in darkness.

A fearless smile appeared on her face. Knowing exactly what she was thinking, I said to her, "Maybe we shouldn't." Three vertical lines creased her forehead.

Paying me no mind, the girl marched up to the gate, grabbed hold of the top with both hands, reared back, and jumped. She swung one foot on top of the crossbar and inched it over to the other side until she was sitting on top of the gate. All she had to do was swing the other leg over to the other side, and she was trespassing on school property.

Straddling the top of the gate as if it were a horse, the girl looked over at me proudly. I had to look down. Her skirt was bunched up to her waist, exposing her bare legs. But she didn't seem the least bit concerned about it.

I heard a thud, and when I looked up, she was on the other side of the gate, her round eyes seeming to say, *Your turn.*

I went up to the gate, put both hands on the crossbar, and jumped over it in one motion. At first, she seemed disappointed at being shown up, but that expression soon faded. "Nice move," she said, and smiled.

We strolled around the schoolyard three times.

"Did you like school lunches back in elementary school?" the girl asked.

"My school didn't have school lunches."

"That's weird. Did you go to private school?"

"Yeah."

"Me? I *hated* school lunches. Everyone in school eating the same thing at the same time . . . don't you think that's kind of creepy?"

"I know what you mean."

"I was watching *Escape from Alcatraz* the other day, and there was a scene where the inmates all have to eat the same thing at the same time that reminded me of school lunches. Do you like Clint Eastwood?"

"Sure. *Pale Rider* is my favorite."

"My favorite has to be *Dirty Harry.*"

The two of us grabbed hold of the horizontal bars in the playground and swayed back and forth like a pair of baby monkeys.

"What kind of music do you listen to?" she asked.

"All different kinds. But I guess I don't listen to a lot of Japanese music."

"Why not?"

"I don't know. I never really thought about it. What kind of music do you listen to?"

"I listen to all different kinds. But I guess I don't listen to a lot of Japanese music."

"Why not?"

"I don't know. I never really thought about it."

"I guess that makes us the same."

"I guess it does."

We strolled over to a bronze bust of some famous person in the corner of the schoolyard and took turns poking our fingers up his nose.

"Any dreams for the future?" she asked.

I thought about it and answered, "If I could, I'd go to a top-tier college, get in with an elite corporation, fly up the promotional ladder, and if I could, marry a pretty girl, have two adorable kids, build a house in the city, retire, and then learn to play Go. If I could, I'd take my wife's hand in mine on a warm autumn day and tell her how happy I was to have spent my life with her and pass away quietly of old age."

"Are you serious? Would you really want to live a life like that if you could?"

"Yeah." I noticed her look down. "Why are you laughing? Did I say something funny?"

"You should hear how the boys I know talk. They all say, 'I'm going to be famous.' They can never tell you in any concrete terms how they're going to get famous, but they're all ready to tell you, 'I'm going to be huge someday.'"

"That's because they're trying to get your attention. They're trying to tell you they're a sure thing."

"Don't you want to try to get my attention?"

I floundered for an answer.

"So why don't you think you'd be able to have a life like you imagined? You could if you really tried, right?"

When I didn't answer, she asked, "What's wrong? Did I ask something I shouldn't have?"

"I'm going to be like Bill Gates someday."

"You can't impress me that way now." She strode off ahead of me.

When I caught up to her, we lay down and sprawled out in the middle of the schoolyard.

"It's so peaceful," she said.

"Yeah."

We gazed at the stars for a while.

"Would you mind telling me your name?" I asked.

"We don't need to bother with names, do we?" she said. I looked over in her direction. She relented and said, "Sakurai."

"What's your first name?"

"I don't want to say. I hate my first name."

"I'm—"

"Sugihara."

"How did you . . . ?"

"I read your mind earlier," said Sakurai, smiling. "But I couldn't read the first name. What is it?"

"We don't need to bother with names."

"I know, right?"

"Yeah."

A shooting star streaked down above us. Its red tail was clearly visible, even in the well-lit sky of Tokyo.

Sakurai shot up into a sitting position. "Did you see that?"

I sat up, turned to her, and nodded.

"This is horrible! I've never been so embarrassed in front of a boy in my life."

"Embarrassed?"

"A shooting star? There's absolutely nothing more embarrassing than gazing up at the sky with a boy and seeing a shooting star. Don't you think?"

"Really?"

"Yeah."

"Really?"

"Yeah. God, you didn't make a wish or anything like that, did you?"

I shook my head. "I didn't have time."

"Oh good!" The lines on her forehead disappeared, and a really sweet smile came across her face. "Please don't tell anyone about the shooting star. It's just too embarrassing. It'll be just our secret."

What would other guys do in this situation?

I wanted to touch her. Anywhere would have been fine. If I could reach out and she didn't spurn my touch, I knew that I could make this restless feeling that was consuming me go away. *I don't want to lose this girl smiling in front of me.* I felt something strong for this girl I barely knew. And I believed that maybe *she* would let me touch her.

While I went back and forth about whether to reach out my hand, she jumped to her feet. "We should be getting back."

Feeling both relieved and heartbroken, I nodded and stood up.

When we got to the gate, she said, "You go first. I want to see you jump from behind." I jumped over the gate in one motion. I waited for her on the other side. She beckoned me back. Assuming she needed help getting over, I reached across the gate with both arms, when suddenly she grabbed hold and drew me in. My body pressed up against the gate. Sakurai's face came closer to mine. "I knew you were a great jumper," she said and pressed her lips against mine. What soft lips. Whatever it was that Sakurai knew about me, I didn't give a damn. At that moment, I couldn't care less.

We stood there with the gate between us and kissed for a while. That restless feeling from earlier had completely vanished.

3

That night, Sakurai and I ended up walking to Tamachi Station.

I bought a newspaper and pen from a kiosk, and we each tore off a piece of the newspaper and wrote down our phone numbers.

"What are you doing next Sunday?" Sakurai asked.

"I'm seeing a friend."

Sakurai's forehead wrinkled. "Are you going out with another girl?"

I hastily shook my head. "I'm just seeing a guy."

She stared into my eyes—hard. "I don't like lies, okay?"

After a short silence, I nodded. Although there were lots of things I hadn't told her yet, I hadn't lied.

We passed through the ticket barrier, and before we went to our respective platforms, Sakurai asked mischievously, "What would you do if I said I really wanted to see you Sunday?"

"I'd go see my friend. He's someone I need to keep my promises to."

"Sounds like he's a really good friend."

"He is."

Now let me tell you about when I was going to Korean school.

Like I said, I received my elementary and junior high school education at North Korean school. I learned Korean, North Korean history, and all about the Great Leader Kim Il Sung. I also learned the kind of stuff they teach in Japanese school, like Japanese, math, and physics.

The Great Leader Kim Il Sung.

If you're going to talk about Korean schools, there's definitely no avoiding this guy. Ever since I was a kid, I'd been given an earful about just how great and honorable he was.

A communist society like North Korea doesn't recognize religion but needs something resembling one to unify its people. Kim Il Sung was that something—the charismatic founder of a religion.

As much as I can explain it now, I definitely couldn't understand it back then, so despite thinking how weird it was to be forced to swear blind loyalty to Kim, I simply accepted it as normal. I had spent my entire childhood in a North Korean school, which, after all, was really an organized religion.

Then one day in the third grade, I came to a realization.

It happened during a lecture titled "Kim's Early Years." The focus of the lecture that day was about how young Kim Il Sung used a slingshot he'd made to attack a Japanese official who'd come to his home to arrest his father for inciting the anti-Japanese movement. The moral of the story was how great Kim Il Sung was—even as a child—but what I thought was this: *we're greater than this guy.*

I was thinking about how the year before, when I was in second grade, I was walking home from school with some friends and a police car came up behind us. Seeing some of us spilling over into the road, the female officer yelled into the megaphone mounted on the police car, "Walk on the side of the road, you pieces of human garbage!"

None of us were particularly hurt by this. There were always right-wing propaganda trucks coming around the school, hurling much worse insults, so we were used to the abuse. We were used to it, sure, but it still pissed us off.

So the next day, we quickly got together a bicycle squad and began a series of guerilla-style attacks on the police. Our mission was simple:

patrol the neighborhood on our bicycles, our baskets loaded with water balloons, and when we found a cop car, bomb them and run.

We succeeded in pulling off one attack after another. We carefully planned our escape route down side streets beforehand. Not once were we caught.

About two weeks into our campaign, a water balloon landed on the windshield of a police car and broke. The kid who threw it had filled the balloon with water mixed with black, green, red, and brown paint. Deprived of a clear view for an instant, the car drifted across the road like a Formula One race car and crashed into the guardrail. After safely escaping the scene, we climbed up onto the roof of an apartment building and watched the aftermath of the accident. One of the two female officers involved in the crash was in tears. We didn't want to be bullies, so we decided to forgive and forget and put an end to our attacks.

By the way, we were never told what happened to Kim Il Sung after he attacked the official with the slingshot. Did he get away with it?

All kidding aside, if Kim Il Sung could walk on water like that other charismatic religious leader guy, I could see myself being so taken with that incredibly tall tale that I might pledge my loyalty to him. But to me, all the stories about the legendary Kim Il Sung were lacking. There was nothing appealing about them. Or exciting. And that's how I came to this realization that day in third grade:

Our stories are better.

After that, my teachers started calling me "the biggest dumb ass since the school's founding." I quit studying, my grades went down the toilet, and I started making up all kinds of ridiculous excuses to stay home from school.

I hated school with a passion. Especially what took place at the end of the school day: general review and self-criticism, the communists' favorite pastime. A typical review or *soukatsu* went something like this. The teacher would single out one student for speaking Japanese in school, make him own up to this offense, and then force him to rat out another student who was guilty of the same. If you refused to talk, you might get smacked. We never blamed anyone for ratting someone else out, though. After all, we were only doing it so we could be dismissed and hang out together after school. As long as this practice of general review and self-criticism continued, I had no intention of accepting communism.

Practices leading up to the annual athletic festival consisted mostly of group exercises. In fourth grade, military-style foot drills were added to our practices. A perfect military march. The practices continued until our rubber-soled shoes could produce the same sound that military shoes made. And before any of us knew it, we had become youth members of the Kim-led Korean Workers Party and were told we'd fight for Kim Il Sung one day. I wanted nothing to do with it.

At school, there was this feeling of being repressed, of being kept under constant and strict control. So around the start of the fourth grade, I began to make up excuses like "the left side of my head hurts" or "the backs of my eyes feel hot" or "I have a splitting tongue-ache" and stayed home from school.

While my father, who was still an enthusiastic member of Chongryon back then, wasn't exactly thrilled with me ditching school, he didn't force me to go either. And since my mother was happy to have me around the house, I skipped school with my parents' approval.

One day, soon after I started fifth grade, my father, who'd seen me watching movies all day, asked, "Isn't there something you'd rather be doing?"

After some thought, I said that I wanted him to teach me to box. I had just watched *Rocky* the other day. The pachinko business allowed my father to keep pretty flexible hours, so my training began the very next day.

The first day, we headed for the big neighborhood park, the one with the running trails. Once we arrived, my father walked straight into the grassy area in the middle of the park. I followed him. When we got to the middle, my father and I faced each other, standing some distance apart. He stared at me for a while, saying nothing.

Just what kind of training did he have in store for me?

I was a little nervous. Then he finally opened his mouth.

"Hold out your left arm," he said. I did as I was told. "Now turn around once."

"Huh?"

"Just turn around once in either direction. Like a compass."

The look on his face was dead serious. I turned around counterclockwise with my arm extended in front of me. When I came around so that I was looking at my old man again, he said, "The circle you made with your fist is roughly the size you are. If you stay inside that circle and take only the things within your reach, you can go through life without ever getting hurt. Do you understand what I'm saying?"

I nodded slowly.

"What do you think about that?"

"I think that's lame," I answered without skipping a beat.

The old man cracked a smile. "Boxing is the act of breaking through the circle with your own fists and taking something from outside it. Outside is crawling with tough guys. And while you're trying to get something, someone else might come inside and take something of yours. It hurts to hit and hurts to get hit. Fighting is a scary thing. Now do you still want to learn to box? You know you're safer staying inside that circle."

I answered without the slightest hesitation. "Yes."

My father cracked another smile. "Then let's get started."

At first, he forced me to run and then run some more.

"The boxing happens above the torso, sure, but a strong punch is generated from strong footwork. A house built on a bad foundation will easily collapse. That's why you run."

After I was able to run the trails without losing my breath, he taught me how to throw a punch. In the beginning, I had a habit of lifting the heel of my pivot foot when I punched.

"Plant your foot. Don't make an enemy of the ground."

Next came footwork. During his fighting days, my father was your typical swarmer—he stood and traded blows with his opponent. So naturally, I expected him to teach me in-fighting techniques. I was wrong. My old man began to move right and left, backward and forward with easy, flowing steps. As I watched in wonder, he stopped and cracked an invincible grin. "Out-boxers don't play well to the crowd. I needed the money. Sometimes you have to lose something to get something back."

At first I kept my knees straight and stiff, so my footwork was leaden.

"Bend your knees a little and keep them moving. Keep your knees loose, and they can absorb the force of a punch. A tree that is unbending is easily broken in a powerful storm. But not grass." Scratching the scar at the corner of one eye he added, "Or so says some guy named Lao Tzu."

His conscience must have nagged him for plagiarizing the Chinese philosopher.

On nontraining days, such as when it was too rainy or when my father had to work, I went with my mother to Ginza and watched a movie. My mother loved watching Hollywood movies on the big screen; afterward, she'd always look at me with her eyes twinkling and say, "Wasn't that good?" I always smiled and nodded no matter how boring the movie.

After the movie, we usually went to Sembikiya or Shiseido Parlour and got something sweet to eat. Although I wasn't exactly a fan of sweets, my mother would look at me with a cherubic smile and say, "Isn't it good?" And I'd smile and nod.

Sometimes I'd think I didn't need school as long as I had my mother and father in my life. Unfortunately, this honeymoon with my parents didn't last. In the middle of the sixth grade, I abruptly hit a rebellious phase.

My last day of training with my father was July 7, the day of the Star Festival. I dragged my feet all the way to the park. My father and I entered the grassy area and stood facing each other.

"Today I'll teach you how to duck into a right-left combination." He smiled. "Ready, Luke?"

The night before, my father had come into the living room where I was watching *Star Wars: The Empire Strikes Back* on video and began to watch along with me—something he almost never did. While he watched the training scenes with Luke Skywalker and Master Yoda, he kept nodding with this look of satisfaction. I had a bad feeling. When the movie ended, my father said, "Luke, you may call me Yoda."

You're Darth Vader, any way I look at you.

And so, there was already an ominous air on this last day of training. And then just as I was about to totally lose it for being called Luke a third time, thick blue clouds began to cover the sky. Thunder rumbled in the distance. Looking up, my father said, "Doesn't look good. Let's get out of here."

Too late. The heavy rain came down upon us as we reached the park exit. My father and I ran back into the park and took cover beneath a great ginkgo tree that looked about three hundred years old. We squatted near the foot of the tree and stared idly at the rain coming down in thick strands. Then my father said in a voice barely audible above the rain hitting the ground, "What do you want to be in the future?"

After a long pause, I answered, "Castro."

The old man gave me a look as if to say, *smart aleck*, and turned his gaze back on the rain. His eyes slowly traced the thick strands upward until he was looking up at the sky. "Seems connected all the way up to heaven," he said in a small voice. "I wonder if heaven really is a good place . . ."

All I could think then was that he must've been knocked in the head one too many times, but in retrospect, I think I understand what he might've been feeling. My father had suffered the loss of one of his exchange booths only a short while before.

The old man dropped his head and inhaled deeply. Then he looked at me and grinned. "Well, my mind's made up," he said. "I'm going to make like a carp climbing up a waterfall and climb right up to heaven. You can come with me if you want!"

He ran out from under the tree, into the hard rain, into the grassy area, and began jumping up and down, jumping toward the heavens. Again and again, beaming from ear to ear. At times, he went into some odd dance steps. Every move was like nothing I'd seen before.

Anyway, seeing as how I was in this rebellious phase, all I could think was, *What is this punch-drunk old man doing?* But his moves might have looked a little like Gene Kelly's dance from *Singin' in the Rain*. That scene never fails to lift my spirits no matter how many times I watch it.

Soon the thick clouds moved on and the rain stopped. The sun appeared and bathed the grass in its warmth. Standing on the grass carpet, my father looked at me with his head crooked a little to the side, as if he were asking a question.

Why didn't you come with me?

After I entered junior high school, I started to go to school regularly again.

I still hated school with a passion. I only went because my friends were there. They were all like blood brothers to me. We expected to go through school with more or less the same students up until high school. It was like going through a long, extended training camp together, which created a bond beyond friendship. And what caused this bond to truly blossom was a nutrient called—you guessed it—prejudice.

This is going to sound like a joke, I know, but every year on April 29 on Emperor Showa's birthday, Japanese students from sports clubs and conservative student groups all over came to our school on a so-called Korean hunt, so we had to walk home in groups. We had to stick together whether we wanted to or not.

Spending every waking minute with this bunch was incredibly comfortable. Not to mention a blast. Though we never said it out loud, none of us believed that we would amount to much, so we might as well live it up while we were in the cradle of school. Although I've never been to Carnival, I understand why the working people of Rio cut loose during Carnival season. In the swirl of Carnival, *they* were the center of attention. The others couldn't even dance the steps.

My friends and I invented all sorts of games, roughhoused until we hurt, and laughed until we couldn't breathe. "Stop laughing like a bunch of idiots," our teachers told us. "Show some awareness and self-respect as North Koreans!"

Sure, I hated school, but surrounded by my group of friends, I had a sense of security. I felt that I was protected by something. Even if that something drew a tight, complete circle around me and choked me to the point of suffocation, leaving that circle required a fair amount of courage.

My parents' trip to Hawaii and Tawake's disappearance turned out to give me the courage I needed.

So now I'll tell you about Tawake's disappearance.

Tawake was a *senpai*—an upperclassman—two years my senior, who ran the 100-meter dash in 11.2 seconds as a third-year in junior high school. He had short, bristly hair that was unbending in the wind even when he ran at top speed. There was a rumor that he'd head-butted someone in a fight and made tiny holes all over the guy's skin. His hair was as coarse as a scouring brush. *Tawashi* (scouring brush) + *ke* (hair) abbreviated became "Tawake."

I called him "Tawake" and in turn he called me "Crazy" and looked after me like a brother.

Right after entering junior high school, a bunch of us first-years were rounded up on Tawake's orders and roped into fighting a motor-cycle gang. There was a strict hierarchy in Korean schools, owing to the influence of Confucianism, and a senpai's orders were absolute.

We glared at each other from a distance. Tawake ordered me, "Go."

Out of my mind with nerves, I answered, "Okay," and took off alone toward the mob. I got the stuffing beat out of me and sustained injuries that took two weeks to recover from.

"Who actually does that?" said Tawake in disbelief. "You're crazy, you know that?"

With that, the nickname "Crazy" stuck throughout my junior high school years.

Tawake was the star striker on the soccer team and something of a legend in our school. I was on the basketball team, but as soon as practice ended, I spent most days prowling the streets with Tawake. We'd go looking for someone to scrap with and fight them. No reason necessary. If we locked eyes and the other guy didn't look away, game on. Tawake and I were always angry. We didn't know why. All we knew was that basketball and soccer alone weren't going to relieve our anger.

Whenever a battle royal broke out against a mob of kids from another school, the police would arrive on the scene and try to chase us down. I always ran in the same direction Tawake did. But it wasn't long before I'd lose sight of his bristly, unbending hair. I could never catch up to him. The police had never been able to catch Tawake.

On the day of Tawake's graduation, I handed him a bouquet of flowers. He smiled bashfully and gave my thighs a gentle kick. "Keep working those legs. We're nothing if we can't run fast."

The last time I saw Tawake was during spring recess of my second year in junior high, a little while before my father confronted me about choosing my country of citizenship. Tawake called me out of the blue, and the two of us went to an *izakaya* and drank. Tawake, who'd gone on to North Korean high school, had grown bigger since I'd seen him last and was now able to run the 100-meter dash in 10.9 seconds.

We caught each other up on the latest news, and when I told him about my father's recent Hawaiian awakening, Tawake laughed his head off. Once he stopped, he asked, "Have you thought about what you're going to do in the future?"

I shook my head.

"Are you thinking about going to Korean high school, graduating, and working at a Korean-owned pachinko parlor or yakiniku restaurant or as a money lender like me? Or are you going to be a doctor or lawyer?"

We looked at each other and laughed. In Zainichi society, this was the fairy tale that parents told their children:

Even North Koreans can take the Japanese national examination and become doctors and lawyers.

But the reality was none of us ever dreamed of being a doctor or lawyer or anything that required a national examination. Lou Reed had our situation exactly right in "Dirty Blvd." People like us don't get to dream. Maybe Lou Reed was Zainichi.

Anyway, none of the people around me wanted to become doctors or lawyers or believed they could ever become one. We weren't raised in a system that made that sort of thing possible. That fairy tale every North Korean parent told their kid sounded like this to my ears: *join a Serie A league soccer club and score a goal.*

Tawake. Now *he* might have been able to score a goal. Although there's not much point in talking hypothetically, if Tawake had been Japanese, he would easily have become a great player in the J League, been scouted by a foreign club, and gotten rich and famous playing in Serie A or the Bundesliga. Tawake was born in Japan, was raised in Japan, and spoke Japanese. He also happened to be a foreigner with North Korean citizenship. It was virtually impossible for a foreigner to reach the J League, much less become rich and famous. Tawake had run into an obstacle that had finally stopped him in his tracks. This was the story Tawake told me around the time three empty beer bottles sat on the table:

"I got fingerprinted awhile back."

Back then, the government still had a fingerprinting system for foreign residents. When you turned sixteen, you had to go to the Alien Registration Office and get your fingerprints taken, like a criminal. I'd already been fingerprinted on one of my "trips" down to the station, but for Tawake, who had never been caught, it was a first.

"I was going to go down to the registration office and punch the daylights out of the bastards. You can get into trouble for refusing to get fingerprinted. I didn't want the hassle, so I figured I'd get at least a little payback by decking the bastards at the office."

Tawake lifted his beer glass to his lips and drained it.

"But when I got there, this old man with a gimpy leg came out. He acted so sorry and kept saying, 'Thank you for coming down,' to me, a kid. He must've said it about fifteen times. And then a girl with this big birthmark on her face brought the fingerprint form and didn't look at me once but shielded my hands with her notebook the whole time so the others couldn't see I was getting fingerprinted. I forgot about punching anybody after that. I must've said sorry about ten times. More times than I've ever said it in all my life."

Tawake looked at me with a serious expression and continued.

"They finally got me. The government's power is a terrifying thing. You have to be pretty fast to outrun it."

Walking back from the izakaya, Tawake drunkenly smacked my head and kept muttering, "Hawaii . . . Crazy . . . Hawaii . . ." He gave me a wobbly kick in the thighs and said, "I'll see ya."

I bowed and began walking away. From behind me, I heard the first word Tawake had ever said to me: "Go."

When I turned around, Tawake had turned around and was already walking in the opposite direction. His hair stood tall and unbending against the wind. That was the last time I saw him.

The story I heard later was that Tawake had switched from North Korean to South Korean citizenship and quit high school before that last night I saw him. Then he was gone. No one knew where he went. According to rumors, he had gone to France and joined a foreign mercenary unit or to England and became a hooligan leader or to Amsterdam, where he became king of the hippies. Wherever he was, I was sure he was running, running so fast that no one could catch him.

As soon as I started my third year in junior high, I announced to my teachers that I was going to take the Japanese high school entrance exams. I expected them to laugh me out of the room—the school's biggest dumb ass shooting his mouth off again—but the school had fallen on hard times. The number of students going to North Korean schools was declining every year, and if this continued, the survival of the school was at risk, so they hated to lose even a single student. But that wasn't what the vice principal called me in to tell me.

"We don't mind if you go to a Japanese school. But what we can't have is the other students hearing about it and getting ideas of their own. So taking the Japanese entrance exams has to remain secret."

And that was how I was given my discharge notice.

The vice principal also said this: "What makes you think you can get into a Japanese high school in the first place? When you come crying back to us, we won't admit you to the high school. Keep that in mind as you study for the exams."

I wasn't particularly hurt by this. Back then, I couldn't even read the English word "certainly," pronounced "George" as "Gerogay," and thought the past tense of "leave" was "leaved." So no, I wasn't particularly hurt by what the vice principal said, but it did piss me off.

I began to study like crazy. I quit the basketball team, saying that my joints were screwed up; quit looking for trouble after school, citing a moral awakening; secretly went to a cram school; and studied like never before. A certain friend spotted me going into the cram school one afternoon, and the next morning it was all over school. Then the bullying by the teachers began.

One day about a month before my high school entrance exams, I was so tired from studying the night before that I fell asleep in the History of Kim Il Sung's Revolution class. I was slapped awake by the teacher's hard palm. The class was stopped midlecture, and after I was made to sit on my heels before the teacher's desk, the teacher ordered me to criticize my behavior. I kept quiet since I couldn't think of anything to criticize, and the teacher struck me again. A metallic ringing filled my ear. It was a familiar sound. My eardrum had burst.

I took three toe kicks in the thigh. It hurt so bad that tears welled up in my eyes. I took five finger-flicks to the bridge of my nose. It hurt so bad that five happy memories flew out of my brain. I was grabbed by the ear and pulled down to the ground. I bit down on my humiliation so hard that blood seeped from my gums.

I was called an "ethnic traitor" and kicked in the pit of the stomach, then called a "sellout" and struck across the face again. I couldn't really understand what that last one meant. I knew the literal meaning of the word, of course, but I just couldn't bring myself to think that I was a sellout. I could sense the incongruity of the label but didn't have the words to express it. Then someone who was able to say exactly what I was feeling appeared, like a superhero.

A voice rose up from the back of the classroom.

"We've never belonged to a country we could sell out."

Sunday.

I arrived at the east exit of Shinjuku Station five minutes before the appointed time and found Jeong-il leaning against the pillar by the ticket barrier, reading a paperback. I snuck up on him and without making a sound, peered over at the book. It was *I Am a Cat* by Soseki Natsume.

"Any good?"

Jeong-il closed the book. "'Is the Spirit of Japan triangular? Is it, do you think, a square? As the words themselves explicitly declare, it's an airy, fairy, spiritual thing,'" he said, reciting a passage from the novel.

"Sounds interesting."

He continued his recitation. "'There's not one man in the whole of Japan who has not used the phrase, but I have not met one user yet who knows what it conveys. The Spirit of Japan, the Japanese spirit, could it conceivably be nothing but another of those long-nosed goblins only the mad can see?'"

Jeong-il smiled at me good-naturedly. I adored Jeong-il's smile.

Jeong-il was born to a Zainichi father and a Japanese mother. His father left when Jeong-il was three and had been MIA ever since.

When it came time for Jeong-il to start elementary school, his mother put him straight into North Korean school. Since North Korean schools were classified as miscellaneous schools, and thus didn't qualify for subsidies, tuition was expensive, but she worked tirelessly to pay it.

Thus, a strange half-Korean, half-Japanese student with South Korean citizenship was born. By the start of fifth grade, Jeong-il was called "the brightest student since the school's founding." And because, in part, we were never in the same class until we entered junior high school, I ("the biggest dumb ass since the school's founding") hardly ever talked to him.

"We've never belonged to a country we could sell out."

46

By the time Jeong-il made that declaration, he had achieved perfect grades and attendance for eight years running, could correctly pronounce "certainly" in English, explain the present perfect tense, and read and write cursive letters. Not to mention he'd never shoplifted, shaken anyone down for money, or gotten in a fistfight. He avoided groups altogether. Jeong-il was always alone. Even the teachers didn't know how to relate to him. None of my other friends tried to get to know him either.

Jeong-il's rebellious declaration on my behalf got him hit by the teacher for the first time. After racking my brain, I bought a PlayStation with what little money I had and gave it to Jeong-il as a thank-you gift. At first, he looked at the console as if he didn't know what to do with it but smiled good-naturedly and said thanks. A teacher found the PlayStation and ended up confiscating it. We both got smacked for that. It was a mistake to give it to Jeong-il at school. Jeong-il and I became friends anyway.

After I was miraculously admitted to a Japanese high school and started going there, I grew farther apart from the friends I used to hang out with. The environments that we lived in had completely changed, of course, and in the end, I had become an outsider to my friends.

Jeong-il had continued into North Korean high school, but we kept in touch. In fact, our friendship grew deeper. We met at least once a month and talked about a whole lot of things. Well, actually we talked a whole lot about the usual topics.

Jeong-il and I went into a café and killed time until dinner.

As soon as we settled into our seats, I pulled out a copy of Stephen Jay Gould's *The Mismeasure of Man* from my backpack and handed it to him.

"My number-one pick this month."

"What is it about?" Jeong-il asked.

"Don't believe scientists pushing the theory of genetic determinism."

"I don't follow."

"Let's say, for example, you and I both have small skulls. Some diabolical scientist lumps us all together and comes out and says all Koreans have small skulls and therefore are stupid. That data could be used to oppress us, which is what happened to blacks and Indians in America."

Jeong-il said, "I'll give it a try." He slipped the book into his bag and then took out another paperback and gave it to me. It was *In Exile* by Takeshi Kaiko.

"It's really cool," said Jeong-il.

Riffling through the pages of the book, I said, "You're always reading novels." I didn't believe in the power of the novel. A novel could entertain but couldn't change anything. You open the book, you close it, and it's over. Nothing more than a tool to relieve stress. Every time I said as much, Jeong-il would say something cryptic like, "A lone person devoted to reading novels has the power equal to a hundred people gathered at a meeting." Then he'd continue, saying, "The world would be a better place with more people like that," and smile good-naturedly.

And then it felt like maybe he was right.

After putting the book in my backpack, I said, "The book you lent me last time—Akutagawa's *Aphorisms by a Pygmy*? It was cool."

A joyful smile spread across Jeong-il's face.

When we finished catching each other up on the latest news, the conversation shifted to university. Although I intended to take the entrance exams, I felt conflicted about it. University was essentially a breeding ground for salarymen, and I had no use for such a place. The reason was simple. Even if I did become a salaryman, my nationality prevented me from becoming company president. Deprived of my greatest ambition from the start, I had no intention of slaving away in the system.

Go

"If you're not going to university what're you going to do?" Jeong-il asked.

"Haven't thought about it. Definitely not work nine to five."

"Then maybe you can take the four years at university to decide."

"Sounds like four random years."

Jeong-il took a sip from his lukewarm coffee and said in a serious tone, "But you *should* live a random life. I mean, your life has already veered off the rails. I wish you'd keep on veering and see where it takes you. You're someone who could pull that off. But you know, that's just me." Jeong-il smiled good-naturedly.

I fidgeted in embarrassment. I'd almost never had the experience of being praised by a teacher. Now I knew the feeling.

After getting into a Japanese university, Jeong-il planned to get his teaching license and become a teacher. For a North Korean school.

"Then why don't you live a random life with me?" I asked.

Jeong-il shook his head. "I'm not the type."

"How could you know that now?"

"Because I do. Those things are already decided from the start."

"You sound like a diabolical scientist."

"No, this is different. What I'm talking about is something like a person's role in life."

"Forget about roles."

"If I did that, I'd stop being me."

I let out a short sigh. "Please don't tell me you're going back to that small circle."

Jeong-il drank the cold coffee and said gently, "Do you remember when you said North Korean school was like an organized religion?"

I nodded.

Jeong-il continued. "I don't know all that much about religion, but if it serves the role of taking in vulnerable people of all kinds, then we definitely need Korean schools."

"Except that I was already *in* it before I had a choice. Vulnerable had nothing to do with it."

"Me, too. But if I'd gone to a Japanese school, I might have been bullied and killed myself."

"No way."

"It's true. I used to get bullied all the time by the boys in my neighborhood. They said all sorts of horrible things, too. If they tried to televise it, all you'd hear is one long bleep."

There was a pause, and then Jeong-il and I laughed. Jeong-il stopped giggling and said, "But when I started going to the North Korean school, I saw tough guys like you jumping around, and then I was just tougher. I didn't care what the bullies in the neighborhood said to me."

Another silence passed between us. Then I said, "It's too bad we weren't friends back then. I would've beat down every one of them."

Jeong-il narrowed his eyes at me as if he were looking at something bright and said, "You know what? You did."

We looked at each other and let out a sheepish laugh.

"It's for kids like me that we need organized religion," Jeong-il continued matter-of-factly. "I'm going to study hard at a Japanese university and come back with the proper knowledge the kids coming up after us will need to break out into the wider world. I want to give them the courage that you guys gave me. I'm going to tell them about you, too. About the ridiculously tough-as-nails senpai that went to their school. You better not disappoint them."

The usual good-natured smile was spread across Jeong-il's face. I fidgeted in my seat again.

"You're going to make a great leader."

Jeong-il chuckled bashfully and said, "The 'organization' is beginning to change since Kim Il Sung died. They're slowly turning an eye toward the outside world. Maybe North Korean schools will have evolved into something better by the time I come back."

When Kim Il Sung died a short while back, I felt nothing. In my mind I had completely closed the book on Kim. Never to be opened again.

I caught a glimpse of the clock on the wall. It was past seven. I grabbed the check and said, "Let's get something to eat."

We went to the yakiniku place on Shinjuku 5-chome.

The restaurant took up the eighth through twelfth floors of a twelve-story building, and Jeong-il and I went up to the entrance on the eighth floor. It was dinnertime on a Sunday night, so the restaurant was packed. As we were jostled by the crowd of customers waiting for tables to open up, the hostess—an elegantly made-up woman wearing a chic black dress with her hair tied back—appeared.

"Reservation for two?"

Although we hadn't made reservations, I answered the woman's question with a nod. She led us to the elevator and got on with us. As soon as the door closed, I said, "You look like the mistress of some Chinese mafia boss."

My mother smacked me on the side of the head. Jeong-il chuckled.

"Nice to see you again, Jeong-il," my mother said.

Jeong-il gave her a proper bow and said, "You're looking as pretty as ever."

With a pleased smile, my mother said, "I have some delicious meat set aside for you, Jeong-il."

The elevator opened on the twelfth floor. As we stepped off, I gave Jeong-il a kick in the stomach.

"Pervy bastard."

My mother led us into a private room in the back with tatami floors, and left. The night view from the windows was beautiful. Naomi-san appeared with cups of tea and warm hand towels just as I had rolled over on my side on the tatami mat and groaned, "Damn, I'm hungry."

She was wearing a really elegant navy kimono. I sprang upright and sat on my heels.

"Welcome. Nice to see you again." The outer corners of her eyes turned slightly downward as she smiled flirtatiously. I nearly melted. I glanced at Jeong-il. His eyes were sagging dreamily at the corners, too. Pervy bastard.

Setting the tea and towels neatly in front of Jeong-il and me, she asked, "So how are my rising Zainichi stars? Studying hard?" Jeong-il and I simultaneously answered yes and nodded deeply. Another heart-melting smile appeared on her face.

Naomi-san and my mother were school friends. In high school, she had been known for her good looks. After graduating, she was chosen to be Miss Ice Cream, Miss Grape, and Miss Goldfish, and she went on to become a fashion model. Since both South Korean and North Korean citizenship got in the way of traveling overseas, she became a naturalized Japanese citizen. She quit modeling before she turned thirty-one. "It's a long story," she explained once when I asked her why she had quit. She looked kind of sexy when she said it. She ended up taking over her father's business managing the yakiniku restaurant. By the way, *Naomi* wasn't an alias or a stage name but her given name. She used to be bullied in North Korean school for having a Japanese name. My mother stepped in and defended her, and they became good friends.

"I hope you're hungry," Naomi-san said.

Jeong-il and I nodded.

"I'll bring your food right out. Just give me a minute."

Naomi-san left the room. With his eyes still sagging downward at the corners, Jeong-il, as if in a dream, said, "You know she's single, right?" I grabbed one of his legs and put him in an ankle lock to awake him. Pervy bastard.

◆ ◆ ◆

By the end of dinner, Jeong-il and I were blissfully stuffed. Naomi-san came back with some lime sherbet for dessert, and she sat down and made herself comfortable. In the most adorable way, she asked me, "Will you tell that story again?" It was a story I'd told many times before, but I just couldn't say no to her.

In the fall after I started high school, my family went to South Korea. The purpose of the trip was to visit my grandparents' grave on Jeju Island. For my father, it was a homecoming fifty years in the making. For my mother and me, it was the first time setting foot on South Korean soil. I went to the grave of my grandparents, who died before I'd ever met them, and laid down some flowers. To be honest, I didn't really feel a whole lot of anything, looking at the grave. It was nothing more than a burial mound.

The incident occurred after we arrived on the mainland. We had dinner at a yakiniku place in Seoul, and afterward we got in a taxi. Actually I got in a taxi by myself. My parents shared a taxi with a middle-aged Japanese couple they got to know at the restaurant. The couple was staying in the same hotel as we were.

On the ride back to the hotel, the fortyish driver spoke to me.

"Are you Zainichi?"

When I answered in Korean that I was, he snorted and curled his lips into a sneer. Many Koreans believe that Zainichi live in Japan in blessed, hardship-free comfort, and some of them zealously take swipes at Zainichi. The taxi driver appeared to be that type.

During the entire ride, the driver kept asking stupid questions: "How old are you?" "What do you think of Korea?" "Can you eat kimchi?" And he snorted every time I answered, as if to mock my Korean pronunciation. The taxi meter steadily ticked higher and higher. So did my anger meter.

The taxi pulled up in front of the hotel. I checked the price on the meter and held out some bills. The driver took the bills from me and flipped the meter lever up. The display on the meter turned to zero. For several moments, I waited. The driver continued to look out the front windshield as if I didn't exist. The taxis pulling into the driveway behind us began honking their horns. The hotel doorman was coming closer to investigate. I had no choice but to say something.

"Give me my change," I said in Korean.

The driver turned slightly toward me and made this thoroughly repulsive face that seemed to say, *Huh?* and my anger meter shot straight to a hundred. I drilled the guy in the back of the head with a right corkscrew punch, yelling, "Die!" in Japanese. The driver's body pitched forward, his face smashing against the steering wheel with a dull whack! *Take that, you bastard.* When he turned around, his face was crimson. The driver began to rant and rave in a deafeningly loud Korean I couldn't understand. That's the problem with Koreans—they're so short-tempered.

The driver opened his door and got out. I got out and quickly readied myself for a rumble. The driver came at me with short, quick steps, his right fist cocked next to his face. He lunged toward me with his entire body, so I sidestepped to the left. His punch whiffed the air, leaving his outstretched body completely open. I landed a right hook to his liver. The driver let out a groan and crumpled to the ground.

Before I could bask in victory, the doorman snuck up on me from behind and got me in a full nelson. Just as I was going to break free, I heard a familiar voice at my back.

"What's going on?"

It was my old man. I tried desperately to get free so I could explain the situation, but I couldn't. My father asked the doorman with the viselike hold what happened. The doorman jabbered in Korean so fast that I couldn't make out any of what he said. The doorman didn't know what had gone on inside the taxi.

My father's face went dark in an instant. His eyes shifted to the driver on the ground and then back to me. He seethed with murderous intent. This was bad. Figuring my first priority was to break out of this nelson hold the doorman had me in, I struggled with all my might—in that instant, the same person that taught me how to throw a liver hook landed a real good one with all his weight behind it.

The first thing I threw up was the grilled *kalbi* ribs. The doorman released my arms and let me fall to the ground. As I was throwing up the bibimbap from dinner, my mother's voice floated above me. "Is something the matter?"

"He tried to get this taxi driver's money and hit him," I heard my father explain.

I managed to wobble to my feet so I could explain what really happened. A huge crowd had gathered around us. Taxi drivers, hotel staff, and patrons were all holding their breath, staring at the shitstorm that had come down on me. And then it got worse.

"You ungrateful boy!"

Along with this rebuke, my mother's palm came flying at me. It connected with my chin at just the right angle to make my neck twist completely sideways, causing me to lose my equilibrium and fall down again—right onto the bibimbap that I'd just thrown up. As if that wasn't enough, I was pelted by the thunderous applause that rained down on me. Somehow I managed to raise my head. The crowd clapped with big, sweeping arm motions like a concert audience after a maestro's performance. The taxi driver was sobbing for joy on my father's chest. Seeing this, the crowd became weepy-eyed. Some were shaking my mother's hand. The applause continued. Now and then, I felt a stab of pain from the hostile stares of the crowd. Korea was a Confucian country.

And then I thought, *I hate all you grown-ups. And Korea can go to hell.*

While I was telling the story, some of the restaurant staff had trickled into the private room with bento boxes to take a late dinner break. And when my mother came in with tea for everyone just as I finished telling the story, the staff put down their chopsticks and clapped. Not knowing why, my mother blinked with a blank look on her face. When the clapping subsided, Naomi-san said quietly, "It's such a good story no matter how many times I hear it."

Really?

Soon after my mother set the tea down and left the room, a guy asked, "Do you have any new stories for us?" The restaurant workers were young—all around the same age—but they were ethnically diverse: there was a Zainichi North Korean, Zainichi South Korean, Chinese, Taiwanese, and Japanese. I don't know what got into me, but I decided to talk about mitochondrial DNA.

"Okay. This story is a little different from the last one. Stay awake, if you can. Mitochondrial DNA is the DNA found in a special part of cells—the mitochondria. It's different from the rest of your DNA. Because mitochondrial DNA mutates at a high rate, leaving behind markers where the mutation has occurred, mitochondrial DNA analysis is a really important way scientists search for the origins of humankind."

Silence. The Japanese girl's hand went up.

"You lost me when you started talking about mutations."

"Basically we all have unique markers passed down from our ancestors, and they'll likely continue to be passed down intact to our descendants. So if you use these markers to trace your roots, you can have one big family gathering."

"What do you mean?" asked the Zainichi South Korean man.

"Well, you know that we were born at the very end of one of countless branches of the family tree. Our great-great-grandfathers and great-great-grandmothers gave birth to our great-grandfathers, and our great-grandfathers and great-grandmothers gave birth to our grandfathers, and our grandfathers and grandmothers gave birth to our fathers, and then our fathers and mothers got busy, and we were born. If you're really bored, you can go all the way back to your great-great-great-great-great-great-grandparents. Anyway, our bodies are encoded with a tremendous variety of genetic data inherited from our ancestors and—"

The Chinese girl took it from there. "If we use these unique markers from mitochondrial DNA, we can trace our roots, right?"

I nodded. "I forgot to tell you before that when mitochondrial DNA is passed on to a child, only the mother's is inherited. In other words, you only need to trace a simple line from mother to grandmother to great-grandmother without having to check the paternal side, so it's easy. Until you finally trace your roots all the way back to a single woman."

"You're right. This story is different from the other one," said Naomi-san.

"The reality is the descendants of this single woman—we're scattered all over the world, and it could get really interesting if we were to all gather in one place. Like maybe you'd turn out to have the same mitochondrial DNA as the president of the United States."

The Zainichi North Korean man said, "I have the same mitochondrial DNA as Brad Pitt. I'm sure of it." Loud boos from the others.

I waited for the boos to die down. "They did this study using mitochondrial DNA and found out that about half of the Japanese living on the main island of Honshu have the mitochondrial DNA that's common in Koreans and Chinese. Only five percent have the mitochondrial DNA found in Japanese.

"About two thousand years ago, a whole lot of these people—the Yayoi—came to Japan from the continent. And before the Japanese knew what was happening, they'd become minorities on the Honshu main island."

"But a Japanese person who has the mitochondrial DNA of Koreans and Chinese is still Japanese," the Japanese girl said.

"Sure, because they were born in Japan, raised in Japan, and have Japanese citizenship. But that's all it is. Just like how if you were born in America, raised in America, and had American citizenship, you'd be an American."

"Our roots aren't bound by citizenship," said Jeong-il.

"So how far back do you have to trace your roots?" the Japanese girl asked. "I mean, we don't have a family tree lying around at home or anything."

Jeong-il said, "Maybe just skip over the stuff in the middle and go straight to the single woman. Back when the single woman was alive, there were no distinctions like nationality or citizenship. Maybe we should think of ourselves as just descendants of that time."

Everyone was deep in their own thoughts.

"Nationality isn't much more than a lease to an apartment," I said. "If you don't like the apartment anymore, you break the lease and get out."

"Can you really do that?" the Japanese girl asked.

"It's written clearly in the Constitution of Japan, Article 22, Paragraph 2. 'Freedom of all persons to move to a foreign country and to divest themselves of their nationality shall be inviolate.' It's my favorite article in the Constitution."

"But," began the Zainichi North Korean man, "even if we know all that stuff, isn't it pointless if the people discriminating against you don't?"

"What matters is that *we* know," I said. "Those ignorant haters who discriminate based on nationality and ethnicity are pathetic. We need to educate ourselves and make ourselves stronger and forgive them. Not that I'm anywhere near that yet."

We all laughed. My mother came into the room and announced, "Time to go back to work."

We all promised to meet again soon, and the staff workers excused themselves. It was getting late, so Jeong-il and I decided to call it a night. Waiting for the elevator, we thanked Naomi-san for treating us to dinner, and she said, "Come back and tell us some more stories." She smiled and gently caressed my cheek.

Thank God I'd studied that stuff. Knowledge is power, as they say. The moment the elevator door closed, I took a pretty serious punch in the ribs from the pervy bastard next to me.

Although it was already pretty late when I got home, I decided to stick to my daily routine.

I changed into my training clothes and went for a run. I ran six miles, shadowboxed for ten three-minute rounds with a minute interval in between, and finished with fifty push-ups and fifty sit-ups.

After doing some stretches to cool down, I took a shower. I admired the reflection of my abs in the mirror until I realized I was acting like a total narcissist.

I went back to my room and began practicing the guitar. I'd learned how to get all the fingers down to play the F chord recently. To finish off the ninety-minute practice, I listened to a CD of Jimi Hendrix playing "The Star-Spangled Banner" at Woodstock. To protest the Vietnam War, where it seemed like only black and brown people were being sent to the front lines and dying, Hendrix played America's national anthem on his guitar like this:

Scree scree screee screee screeee screeee
Waaah waaah grraaah grraahh
Squeee squeee squeee
Gagagaaah gagagaaah gaah gaah

It was an awesome sound no matter how many times I heard it. The voices of minority people had no way of reaching the top, so they had to find some way of making their voices louder. Someday I might want to play the national anthem of this country and shred like Hendrix did. I was practicing the guitar for precisely that moment.

I sat down at my desk. After flipping through the Green Beret combat manual, I closed my eyes and simulated a combat situation in my head. Three enemies down.

I was pretty sleepy by then, but I decided to run through my nightly studies. I'd been reading up on the monoethnic myth that's been tossed around in Japan for ages. The lessons were delightful. I learned about how scholars and politicians from back when the word "DNA" hadn't even existed spouted off colorful lies to discriminate against other ethnic groups.

I read through the materials I'd gathered from the library, trying to understand how this monoethnic myth worked. Just the vocabulary and euphemisms made my head hurt:

Monolithic, discrimination, assimilation, expulsion, pure blood, mixed blood, foreign, homogeneity, crossbreed, Yamato people, barbarians, bloodline, Emishi, Kumaso, Ryukyu, national polity, nationality, exclusionism, purity, emperor-centered historiography, Japanese expansionism, unbroken Imperial line, Greater East Asia Co-Prosperity Sphere, national prosperity and defense, universal brotherhood, Japan and Korea as one, Japan–Korea single ancestry, Japan–Korea annexation, Japanization, subjects, governor general, *soshi-kaimei*, territorial possession, empire, colonization, unification, invasion, subjugation, puppet, submission, oppression, control, subordination, isolation, segregation, miscegenation, mixed residence, mixing, indigenous, going to America, difference, prejudice, diversity, propagation, reproduction, alien race, inferior race, superior race, blood relative, expansion, territory, rule, exploitation, plunder, patriotism, eugenics, compatriot, class, heterogeneous, union, unity, collusion, antiforeign, exclusion, removal, massacre, extermination . . .

Screw it. I decided to become Norwegian.

I'd need money. I was banging around the room, trying to dig up anything worth selling, when my father opened the door.

"What time do you think it is?"

"Knock."

"Don't be a jerk."

He sat down on the bed. I ignored him and went about my task.

"What are you doing?" he asked.

"Getting out of Japan. Going to Norway."

"What's got into you all of a sudden?"

"I'm going to Norway and become Norwegian. I'll learn to speak Norwegian and forget this ugly Japanese language. I'm done with this place. And I'm going to—"

"Calm down."

"I'm going to marry a cute Norwegian girl and have a cute biracial daughter and build a happy family."

"So you've given it some thought. But why Norway?"

"I'm getting as far away from Japan as I can."

"The other side from Japan is South America."

"I hate the heat."

"You *have* given it some thought."

My father reached for the pile of books I'd stacked on the floor and picked up *Thus Spoke Zarathustra* off the top.

"What do you know about Nietzsche?" he asked.

"I know some."

"I heard he was a little funny in the head. Did you know that?"

"Better that than a womanizer with a saint complex."

Suddenly I felt the old man's menace in the air.

"Don't talk bad about Marx," he said. "He's a good guy."

I didn't want to get hit, so I decided not to talk back. He watched me work. The menace was gone. Creeped out by the silence, I stopped what I was doing and looked at my father. He had a serious look on his face. Our eyes met.

"*No soy coreano, ni japonés, soy un nómada desarraigado,*" he muttered.

"Huh?"

"It's Spanish. I always wanted to be a Spaniard."

I didn't reply.

"But it didn't work out. Turns out, it wasn't about speaking the language."

"Language has everything to do with your identity—"

"In theory maybe," he said, cutting me off. "But we live in circumstances that can't always be explained away by logic. You'll understand someday."

I sat down at my desk. The old man got up from the bed and came closer. After looking through some of the papers spread out on the desk, he said, "Not a bad thing to know something about darkness. You can't talk about light without some knowledge of darkness. Like your buddy Nietzsche said, 'He who fights with monsters should look to it that he himself does not become a monster. And if you gaze long into an abyss, the abyss also gazes into you.' Keep that in mind."

He stared in the direction of the window behind me as he spoke. I turned around, expecting to find a crib sheet taped to the window. But there was nothing there. Only the dead of night.

When I turned back around, my father delivered a punch that glanced off my cheek as if to caress it.

"You've been acting testy lately. I'm not saying you need to get into trouble like you used to, but you should go out more. Like your buddy Nietzsche said, 'Any man in his youth should apply himself to amusement to his heart's content. Too long a time in a forest of words will leave him trapped and unable to escape.'"

"You made that up."

My father let out a chuckle and tossed the papers back on the desk.

"Go to sleep."

As he moved off, I asked, "What did you say in Spanish before?"

My father picked up the pen on the desk and wrote something down.

"Look it up yourself."

Just as my father got to the door, I asked, "Why did you want to be Spanish?"

He turned around and answered with a straight face, "I heard there were lots of beautiful women in Spain."

On his way out the door, he began to sing the Beach Boys' "Hawaii."

Jackass.

I gathered the books and papers off the desk and set them down on the floor. I decided to keep them there for now. Then I decided to think about Sakurai until I fell asleep.

4

I called Sakurai for the first time on Friday night, exactly a week after the night we met. As soon as she answered, she said, "Working women in America have something like a manual for how not to get played by men, and one hard-and-fast rule is to always turn down a date offer that comes later in the week."

I hadn't even asked her out yet. I was meaning to, of course. "Why's that?"

"Because men are busy asking out their top choice earlier in the week. When they strike out, they go, 'Hey, she'll do' and call the fall-back girl later in the week. Women have to say no when that happens, or they'll be seen as convenient. See?"

I didn't reply.

"Not that I mind because I hate rules like that."

Of course she minds. I'm sure of it. "Next time I'll be more careful."

"Don't forget."

I knew it.

Our date was set for Sunday.

Sunday.

I arrived at our meeting place at the east exit of Shinjuku Station exactly at one. Sakurai was nowhere in sight. I stood off to the side of the ticket entrance and waited.

Ten minutes passed. Anticipating a long wait, I bought a *Newsweek* at the kiosk and began to read. As I became absorbed in an interesting article about a former commando in the North Korean Special Operation Force who was a personal bodyguard to King Sihanouk of Cambodia, something slammed softly into me. The collision had a familiar sensation.

I looked up, and there was Sakurai's unguarded smile.

"Sorry I'm late."

"This hardly counts as late."

Her smile grew wider, and she asked, "So what do you want to do?"

I realized after I'd hung up the phone the other night that we'd only agreed to meet and hadn't discussed what we were going to do. All we wanted to do was to see each other. Before I could suggest seeing a movie, Sakurai spoke first.

"I don't want to walk around Shibuya, which is always packed like a train, or get matching tattoos on our arms to commemorate our first date or go to a bad Italian restaurant whose only claim to fame is that it's always crowded or sing karaoke inside a tiny doghouse of a box. Definitely not."

I hastily shook my head. "I wasn't thinking any of those things. Although I was thinking about going to a movie or something."

"Is there a particular movie you'd like to see?"

"Not especially."

"Then let's do something else."

"Okay, what?"

"Do you want to come with me?" she asked as though it were a challenge.

I nodded.

"Then let's go," Sakurai said and pointed to the ticket machines. We started walking in that direction. I rolled the *Newsweek* into a cylinder and held it in one hand. Sakurai said cheerfully, "Looks like a club. Are you going to protect me?"

I tossed the magazine at the trash bin some distance away. It went in. "I don't need a club to do that."

Seemingly happy, Sakurai body-checked me with all her might. I staggered from the impact. Sakurai looked at me, her brows furrowed.

"Maybe we'll need that club back."

Sakurai and I took the train halfway around the Yamanote Line loop and got off at Yurakucho.

After exiting the station, Sakurai headed toward Hibiya. Dressed in a purple jacket and white skinny jeans with a pair of beige hiking boots, she breezed down the office-lined street. Wearing a black jacket, white T-shirt, regular jeans, and loafers, I silently trailed after her.

We wound up at a corporation-run art museum on the top floor of a building near Hibiya moat. Sakurai entered the building as if she'd been there many times and boarded the elevator. I had never been to an art museum before. But I liked looking at art books. Jeong-il lent them to me.

"Do you come here a lot?" I asked as soon as we got on the elevator.

She shook her head. "My first time. I've always wanted to come here but felt weird going in alone. Are you having second thoughts?"

I shook my head.

When the elevator opened at our floor, Sakurai walked straight up to the ticket booth and bought her own ticket. Before I had a chance to pay.

Featured in the exhibit were painters who'd made their name in the French art world. There were some pretty impressive names: Rouault, Braque, Chagall, Picasso, Dali.

"See anyone you like?" asked Sakurai upon entering the exhibit.

"Rouault and Chagall."

"Who're they?" She smiled playfully. "I don't know the first thing about art."

The way Sakurai and I looked at art was a contrast in styles. I stopped and studied each and every painting. Sakurai, seemingly knowing her likes and dislikes at first glance, stood rapt in front of paintings she liked and blew right past the ones she didn't. It was all so clear-cut and refreshing. I decided to do the same.

I stopped only at Rouault's *The Old King* and Chagall's *The Poet Reclining*. Working my way through the exhibit in this way, I gradually closed the distance between me and Sakurai, who'd been quite a bit ahead of me.

She was standing before a Dali painting, smiling. The name of the work she was admiring was *The Atavism of Dusk*, a reimagination of Millet's *Angelus*. It might've been called a reimagination, but to my eyes, it was just a hideous parody. The couple giving prayer to the dusk—the man had a skull for a head and the woman had something like a spear sticking out of her body. And the country landscape had been turned into desolate rocks.

"Isn't it great?" Sakurai asked as she turned to me.

I gave her a vague nod. She frowned, dissatisfied by my reaction. She spent a lot of time in front of the Dali paintings. At times, she giggled as she leaned so far over the barrier that her nose nearly touched the paint; other times she let out a sigh. I stared at Sakurai the whole time. Watching her never grew old.

Sakurai stopped before the last of the Dali paintings and said, "It's like the artist is picking a fight with me. Provoking me, like, 'You think you understand this painting?'"

This last painting was of a human body made of a series of drawers. Some were opened, some closed.

"I don't understand it at all, but what I do know is that the artist is trying to push my buttons, and my heart is pounding. See?"

Saying this, Sakurai grabbed my hand, pulled it closer, and pressed my palm to her chest. She wasn't kidding. Her heart was racing. Then she put her palm against the middle of my chest.

"Yours is pounding too, Sugihara."

Her heart beat even faster. Mine was beating even faster, but that was because people were beginning to gather around us and stare.

Sakura and I pulled back our hands almost simultaneously and retreated from the Dali painting. She was chuckling happily. I was so embarrassed that in an attempt to distract her, I said, "I read in the papers the other day that Dali is really popular with elementary school boys now."

She said, "Oh yeah?" and was smiling until suddenly she wasn't. She punched me lightly in the ribs.

"Excuse me for having the artistic taste of a school boy."

I bought two programs at the booth near the exit and handed one to Sakurai. She thanked me and took the program. "That was fun," she said.

I nodded earnestly.

We went to Hibiya Park and after walking around for a while, sat down on a bench and let time pass idly by. It was a pleasant spring evening.

"Can I ask you something?" asked Sakurai.

"Sure."

"What's your family like?"

"There's three of us. My parents and me. What about you?"

"We're four. My parents and an older sister. Where is your rural hometown?"

"I don't have one. You?"

"My father's family home is in Kansai, and my mother's is in Kyushu. What does your father do?"

"He's . . . just a humble independent businessman. What about your father?"

"Just a humble salaryman. How many girls have you gone out with?"

"One."

"When was that?"

"My second year of junior high school. For a month."

"Ooh, that's short. Why did you break up? You don't have to answer if you don't want."

"I don't mind. I blew off a date and poof! That was it."

"Why did you blow it off?"

"A buddy asked me to go on a trip. It was at the same time as my date, and I chose to go with my buddy."

"Whatever," she said in disgust. "Why would you do something like that?"

"That's just the way guys are in junior high," I said, lamely. "You have to choose your buddies over your girlfriend. Any guy who chooses his girlfriend over his friends will get himself branded as a traitor. He'll be persecuted."

"That's so stupid."

"You're right."

"Where did you go anyway?"

"Nagoya."

"What for?"

"Sightseeing."

"That's weird."

My friend and I rode the local train to Nagoya, having sworn to each other that we would conquer the parlors of Nagoya and return to Tokyo as pachinko kings. The trip was a blast. With our winnings, we stayed at a hotel, ate some fantastic miso udon noodles, and sat in the first-class car on the bullet train back to Tokyo. We went on a school day, of course. My father decked me when I got home.

"Your girlfriend must have been angry," said Sakurai.

"After she ignored me for two weeks, she called me a loser."

Sakurai said, "Well, of course," and punched me in the shoulder. The conversation stalled. As I searched for something to talk about, Sakurai suddenly began to talk.

"I've been out with three boys. The first was when I was in fifth grade—a boy in the same class, with round eyes. He looked a little like Tom Cruise. I broke up with him because he didn't give me anything for White Day. I was young then. The next one was in my second year of junior high school. It was a boy a year above me—he was captain of the swim team and class president. We broke up after he invited me to his house one Sunday and—with a straight face—handed me a red racing swimsuit and asked me to put it on. I slapped him really hard and stormed out of there. Thinking back on it now, I guess I could've worn the swimsuit for him. He'd probably become a little unbalanced from the pressure of being captain of the swim team and class president at the same time. He was such a serious student. He had a tiny bald spot behind one ear—from the stress, I guess. The third boy was when I was in the first year of high school. He was a college student at Keio University, the son of a lawyer. A really horrible guy, really stupid. He'd say stuff like 'The people around me are such imbeciles.'"

"Why did you go out with a guy like that?" I said, asking the obvious.

"I had a weakness for confident men back then," she said plainly. "Every girl goes through a phase at least once when she's vulnerable to confident men."

"Oh."

"I broke up with him after two weeks," she continued. "Because a foreigner stopped us on the street in Roppongi and tried to speak to us in English."

"What do you mean?"

"The man was probably asking for directions. Anyway, he comes up to us and says 'Excuse me' in English. My boyfriend is all smiles and confident up until 'Excuse me,' but soon all these difficult words come flying out of the man's mouth, and my boyfriend's eyes start jumping everywhere. I half expected smoke to come out of his ears. He noticed me staring at him and somehow managed to regain his confidence and said to the foreign man—what do you think he said to him?"

"I can't imagine," I said.

"He said, 'Ah-hah.' Real confident. 'Ah-hah.' Like that. That's when I realized. This guy was an idiot."

She was giggling, saying this, but I couldn't bring myself to laugh. I prayed never to be spoken to by a foreigner while I was with Sakurai.

"All he needed to say was, 'I can't speak English,'" she added, still smiling.

I made a mental note. A hint of mischief came into Sakurai's eyes.

"Don't you want to ask how far I went with these boys?"

After some wavering, I shook my head. "Knowing will only upset me."

A tender smile came over her face. She said, "Don't be stupid," and punched me hard in the shoulder. As I was smarting from the pain, a dog appeared and trotted toward us. The mutt approached us, gently wagging its tail. Just as I was leaning down to pet its head, Sakurai let out a low growl. *Grrr!* The dog stopped in its tracks, and after flopping its ears forward, gave us a look like *Sorry to have bothered you* and trotted back disappointedly from where he came. I gave Sakurai a look. She said, "Keep all buttinskis at bay. That's a hard-and-fast rule of dating," and smiled sweetly.

After heading out of the park, we went to a CD shop. I recommended Sakurai buy Bruce Springsteen's *Tunnel of Love*, an album I especially liked. The album Sakurai said I should buy was one by a jazz pianist named Horace Parlan called *Us Three*. I had never listened to jazz before.

"My father likes jazz, so I grew up listening to it," explained Sakurai, holding up the CD. "This is really cool."

We wandered around Ginza, stopped at a diner we spotted along the way, and had dinner there. Then we enjoyed an after-dinner stroll to Kachidoki Bridge. We smelled the sea air.

"Wouldn't it be nice to go to the beach? And see the ocean?" said Sakurai.

I nodded. "We should go sometime, soon."

We said goodbye at Yurakucho Station. Sakurai let out a quick "See you" and disappeared up the stairs to the train platform. I went up the stairs to the opposite platform with the same disappointed gait of that dog in the park. I stopped at a random spot on the platform and was looking down at nothing when I noticed a shadow above my vision moving frenetically on the opposite platform. I looked up.

Sakurai was standing on her tippy toes, hopping almost, and waving at me. The eyes of the passengers on both platforms were trained on me. As I stood there, frozen and unable to respond, I could sense the crowd's irritation. The loudspeakers announced an arriving train, and I could hear people clicking their tongue at me. Fighting back my embarrassment, I raised a hand and waved to her. I felt the relief of the crowd. The train pulled into Sakurai's side of the platform, putting her out of sight. I casually lowered my hand and hastily moved from where I'd been standing. People looked on as if they were watching a grandson taking his first steps.

When I got home, I found my mother playing chess with my father in the living room. She'd come home.

"Were you out on a date?" my mother asked, advancing her queen. "Check."

My father said, "I'm in trouble," but he seemed to be in awfully high spirits thanks to my mother's return.

"No comment," I answered.

"Just don't do anything irresponsible," said my mother.

"I know."

My father looked up from the chessboard. He was smiling, his eyes sparkling like those of a kid on the first day of summer vacation. "I can't win," he said to me. "There's no way out. She's just too good."

I knew he'd been lonely, but this was pathetic.

After I completed my daily routine, I listened to *Us Three*. It was really cool. I listened to it three times all the way through before falling asleep.

The next day, Kato, whom I hadn't seen since his birthday party, showed up at my classroom during lunch period.

"Heyyy, lover boy," he said, sitting in the seat next to me.

"Jeez, what happened to your face?" I asked.

Kato's face was darker, like he had a tan.

"My father gave me a trip to Guam for my birthday. It was awesome."

"What a blessed life you lead," I said sarcastically.

"So," Kato began, a smirk plastered on his face. "Did you do it yet?"

"You asking me to rearrange your nose again?"

Kato put a hand to his nose and snapped into a defensive position. "Come on. Give me a break."

"Do you even know who she is?" I asked.

His hand still on his nose, Kato shook his head.

"I was curious, so after you two left the party, I asked around, but no one knew who she was. So you can relax. If no one in my crew knows who she is, that has to mean she's a proper girl. How did you meet up with a cute girl like that anyway?"

"I'm not exactly sure. She's pretty mysterious. She just suddenly appeared and pulled me into her world."

Kato lowered his hand from his nose and said with a straight face, "Maybe she's a snow spirit. Or a crane you once saved coming back to repay the debt in human form, like in the folktale."

"The inside of your head must've dried up from being out in the sun too long."

"Hey, I was born this way," Kato said. "If you're curious, I can do some digging for you. She's in high school, right? If I know where she goes, I can pretty much find out anything through my connections."

I wavered for a moment and shook my head. "Nah. Whoever she is, it doesn't matter."

"Yeah, you're right," Kato said, looking happy for some reason. "This all sounds like a lot of fun, like something out of the movies."

"So long as it doesn't turn out to be a mystery or a suspense thriller."

The bell chimed the end of lunch period. Kato rose from his seat.

"As an objective viewer, I'd prefer seeing a horror or occult film. It'd be exciting to see your wiener get lopped off or something." Kato patted me on the shoulder. "Best of luck."

Calling Sakurai every Monday night became part of my weekly routine. Sometime after the Golden Week holidays, calling Sakurai became a part of my daily routine.

We spent most of our days off together. As we continued to see each other, a certain understanding grew between us. We each had to find cool things the other would like.

We recommended all kinds of books, CDs, and movies to each other and classified them simply according to whether they were cool or uncool.

Sakurai tended to rate most of the things I recommended as cool. Bruce Springsteen, Lou Reed, Jimi Hendrix, Bob Dylan, Tom Waits, John Lennon, Eric Clapton, Muddy Waters, Buddy Guy . . . but Neil Young just wasn't her cup of tea. I asked her why.

"He's not a good singer."

I thought most of the things Sakurai recommended to me were cool. Miles Davis, Bill Evans, Oscar Peterson, Cecil Taylor, Dexter Gordon, Milt Jackson, Ella Fitzgerald, Mozart, Richard Strauss, Debussy . . . but John Coltrane just wasn't my cup of tea. She asked me why.

"Too dark."

My recommendation of Bruce Lee's *Fist of Fury* became one of her favorites. I wound up taking a lot of roundhouse kicks in the leg thanks to that movie. Sakurai's recommendation of *One Flew Over the Cuckoo's Nest* became one of my favorites. After I told her so, I got stuck having to watch more than my fill of Jack Nicholson films. Sakurai really liked Jack Nicholson. I asked her why.

"He's strange and cool."

Sakurai was strange and cool, too.

Books were a pretty weak field for me. Because I hardly read any novels and only read dense books about anthropology, archaeology, biology, history, and philosophy, it was hard to recommend a book that anyone else would find interesting. The novels I'd read based on Jeong-il's recommendation were generally old Japanese novels that Sakurai had already read. Sakurai had been influenced by her book-loving father. She'd read a lot of books.

I read all kinds of novels that Sakurai recommended to me. John Irving, Stephen King, and Ray Bradbury became some of my favorite novelists. But I especially liked James M. Cain's *The Postman Always Rings Twice* and Raymond Chandler's *The Long Goodbye*. When I told Sakurai so, she said proudly, "I knew you'd like them."

There were also things that we "excavated" together. Dashiell Hammett, Sillitoe, Jack Finney, Raymond Carver, *Chariots of Fire*, *Purple Noon*, *The Trouble with Harry*, *Days of Wine and Roses*, *The Wild Bunch*, Elvis Costello, R.E.M., T. Rex, Donny Hathaway, the Kronos Quartet, Henryk Górecki, Terence Blanchard, Egon Schiele, Andrew Wyeth, J. M. W Turner, Roy Lichtenstein . . .

This excavation work was incredibly fun. Our method was simple: walk into a bookstore or CD shop or video rental store together and go with our gut instinct. That was it. We looked at the book cover or CD jacket or video cover art and chose whatever "spoke" to us. But our gut instinct turned out to be your basic .300 hitter. There were strikeouts and lots of easy grounders and fly outs, not to mention lots of time and money wasted. The excavation work was fun anyway.

On the first Sunday of June, we were in a fast-food chain in Ginza when Sakurai asked out of the blue, "Do you want to come back to my house now?"

I didn't know how to answer, so Sakurai added, "We have a media room because of my father's many hobbies. We can listen to music and watch movies together there. That way, we can talk about what we thought right after."

"Won't your father mind if you bring a guy home?"

"My family is completely cool about stuff like that," said Sakurai, giving me a tight-lipped smile. "My older sister is always bringing home her boyfriends for dinner."

Sakurai was looking at me with serious eyes.

I nodded. "Yeah, okay."

Sakurai let out a sigh of relief. "I didn't know what I'd do if you said no."

Sakurai's house was in an upscale residential area in Setagaya.

Sakurai's father had a tuft of hair parted in the middle. He was wearing an expensive-looking denim shirt and nicely faded jeans. He looked at his daughter's male friend without batting an eye, smiled gracefully, and said, "Welcome."

I was shown into the living room and took a seat on the cushy sofa. The mother, with the same look of refinement as Sakurai, appeared with a tray. As she set cups of tea on the table, she said, "Welcome. Please look after our daughter," and excused herself from the living room.

"Where do you go to school, Sugihara-kun?" the father asked.

I told him the name of my high school, to which he said, "Hmm," and added, "It must be a very good school."

I told him truthfully, "Not at all."

Sakurai, sitting next to her father, let out a chuckle—a tiny one, so as not to be too noticeable.

I guess Sakurai's father loved to talk. For a while, he talked my ear off about a lot of different things. He was a graduate of Tokyo University. He was involved in the student protest movement in the late sixties. He was a salaryman at a famous trading company. He really loved jazz. He called black people "African Americans." He called Indians "Native Americans." He hated Japan.

"Do you like this country, Sugihara-kun?" he asked, as soon as Sakurai left to use the bathroom. I didn't know how to answer, and he continued. "I have flown around the world on business, and I've never seen a more unprincipled country than this one. It's enough to make me ashamed to call myself Japanese overseas. To express my active rejection of the Japanese government, I refuse to participate in elections. If I have time to go vote, I'd rather spend that time with my family. Doing so will ultimately make Japan—"

"Are you"—I cut in—"familiar with the meaning of the name Japan?"

The father, with a deflated look, gave some thought to my question and answered, "It's the land of the rising, isn't it?"

"That's one theory, but apparently there are lots of others. The theory that *hi no moto*, or the sun's origin, which is a common epithet for Yamato, eventually turned into the country's name is one example. Scholars are still debating over it. One book that I read recently said that Japan is a rare country whose citizens grow up knowing nothing about how their country's name was derived because it's completely overlooked in history education."

I was babbling.

Sakurai's father stared at me with a look that seemed to ask, *So?* Suddenly, I was hit with a feeling of futility. *What am I doing here?* And then the answer came into view. Sakurai returned from the bathroom and, without sitting down again, told her father, "I think it's time to give Sugihara some space."

As we left and headed for the media room, Sakurai asked in a low voice, "Too annoying?"

Shaking my head, I told her, "Not at all." It was the first lie I ever told her.

The media room was in the basement, a ten-tatami room with finely grained wood flooring. It was equipped with a very expensive-looking stereo and speakers and a projector and a giant screen. Hundreds of CDs, LPs, and DVDs lined the built-in shelves along the walls. Taking up the center of the room was the same sofa as the one in the living room.

Sakurai put Mozart's Symphony No. 25 in the CD cradle and sat on the sofa. She saw me staring at the words on the spine of the CD case and said, "Come over here," while patting the cushion next to her. I sat down on the sofa, leaving a small space between us. Sakurai picked up the remote and turned on the CD player. The symphony blared from the speakers.

After some time passed, Sakurai tapped me on the shoulder. Her mouth was opening and closing. But I couldn't hear her. At first, I thought I couldn't hear because of the deafening music, but quickly realized that she wasn't making a sound on purpose. Her mouth kept repeating the same movements. Watching her lips go from one shape to the next, I could hear the three words in my head. *I. Like. You.* I reached out and put my hand on the nape of her neck. Her lips stopped moving. I tensed my hand behind her neck and pulled her toward me. We must've kissed for about ten minutes. We didn't unlock lips once until the symphony's first movement ended.

When we came out of the media room, dinner was waiting upstairs. Before I could protest, I was seated at the table. Sakurai's older sister was there, too. She was giving me a serious once-over, ignoring all pretense of restraint.

"Itadakimasu." Let's eat.

Dinner began. It occurred to me that this was my first time eating with a Japanese family. After this realization, I became so nervous that the chopsticks felt a little heavy in my hand. Sakurai, maybe thinking I was nervous for a different reason, brought up all sorts of cheerful topics to try to ease the tension and filled the dinner table with laughter.

Sakurai's parents and older sister were really friendly people. I laughed a lot at their stories and occasionally joined in the conversation. Before I knew it, I even found my appetite.

Noticing Sakurai's father filling his glass a couple of times with iced tea, I asked, "Do you not drink?"

"None of us here can drink alcohol." Sakurai answered instead. "Even a sip will knock us out cold."

"Do you drink much, Sugihara-kun?" Sakurai's sister asked, smiling meaningfully.

"I'm still underage." I answered with a serious face, which prompted a short laugh. "Apparently people with innately low alcohol tolerance exist only in the Mongoloid race."

Everyone in the family nodded with mild interest. I was going to explain why but decided against it.

"What's the difference between someone who can drink and someone who can't?" Sakurai asked.

"When you consume alcohol, a toxic compound called acetaldehyde is created and makes you feel drunk. Someone with a high tolerance doesn't get drunk because the ALDH2 enzymes in their body work to break down the acetaldehyde. But not in someone with low tolerance. Their ALDH2 enzymes don't."

After listening to my explanation, Sakurai's father nodded his satisfaction and said, "Like I said, you must go to a very good high school."

Sakurai and her older sister chuckled quietly to themselves. I guess Sakurai had talked to her sister about me.

When we were ready to leave the house, Sakurai's father saw us off at the door and said, "You're welcome anytime."

Sakurai seemed happy the whole time we walked back to the train station. When we stopped at the ticket barrier to say goodbye, she said, "I think my father liked you."

I nodded vaguely. Looking down a bit, she said, "My father isn't exactly stylish but he's not a bad guy. He's really sweet and understanding."

I playfully feigned a punch, just touching Sakurai's left cheek. She raised her head and looked at me.

"I'm really glad if your father liked me," I said.

"Really?"

I gave her a firm nod. Sakurai let out a relieved sigh and smiled bashfully.

"So I noticed your family didn't call you by your name."

Sakurai said cheerfully, "That's because I warned them not to."

"It'd be nice to know eventually," I said.

"Mysterious, isn't it?" Sakurai narrowed her eyes into that challenging look of hers. "I guess I'll tell you eventually."

Ever since that first visit to Sakurai's house, most of our dates took place there. Sakurai and I spent a lot of time in the media room.

Once we spent the whole day watching all three movies in the Godfather series. The Godfather trilogy meant a lot to me. In the opening of *The Godfather: Part II*, the scene with young Vito Corleone arriving on Ellis Island and looking at the Statue of Liberty has got to be the most beautiful scene I have ever seen in movies.

I'd become convinced that as long as there are immigrants and refugees in this world, the Godfather movies will live on. When I stressed this to Sakurai, she said, smiling, "I don't know if I understand completely, but I know that you really love *The Godfather*, Sugihara."

Another time we listened to a bunch of Miles Davis recordings. Sakurai lectured me about the importance of Miles Davis in jazz history. While we listened to Miles's greatest recordings, from bebop and cool to hard bop, modal, and funk, in that order, she gave me a detailed explanation. She ended her lecture with, "Miles *is* jazz." I pulled her close and kissed her.

Other times, we spent the entire day caressing each other. We touched and kissed each other gently while our favorite music played. But we didn't touch each other down there. We had a silent understanding that this wasn't the place we were going to give ourselves completely to each other. We were both fearful that if we went too far, our desires would get the better of us, and we might violate that understanding.

I kissed the nape of Sakurai's neck while gently caressing her back. Sakurai preferred being kissed on the nape of the neck rather than on her breasts. When I ran my fingers over the curves of her back, she'd let out a deep and heavy breath. Then she'd whisper into my ear repeatedly: "You're amazing."

Sakurai liked to kiss my muscles. Her favorites were my biceps, deltoids, and abdominals. Sometimes, she'd bite down on my biceps and growl. Sakurai always planted a kiss on every square of my six-pack.

The first time we took off our tops, there was an odd moment when we'd finished caressing each other. Maybe embarrassed by having to put our clothes back on, we got dressed in silence. A Brahms piano concerto was playing. I finished dressing first, so I asked a question to fill the awkward silence.

"I wonder what country Brahms was from."

Sakurai stopped for a moment after fastening her bra and said, "I'm not sure. But I don't think it really matters where he's from. People all over the world appreciate Brahms."

I went up to Sakurai and leaned my body against her, gently pushing her down on the sofa. I rested my head on her chest, with my right ear down. The sound of music died, and I could only hear Sakurai's heartbeat. Sakurai's heart didn't beat at the same steady pace, but was always changing. She gently patted the top of my head and kissed it three times.

It was a ritual we went through after we had finished caressing each other. I would listen to Sakurai's heartbeat, and she would kiss the top of my head three times. Then we would leave the media room, reluctantly.

Sakurai and I wanted every bit of each other. There was no mistaking it. But the place where we were going to give ourselves completely to each other had to be special. We concluded that we would go somewhere with a beautiful view of the ocean. And that going there with our parents' money wouldn't be cool. We were going to go someplace special with money we'd made ourselves and give ourselves to each other. Where that place was or how much money we'd need to get there, neither of us had any idea. We decided to get started anyway. Summer vacation was coming up. We decided to cut back on seeing each other and put our energies into part-time work.

I spent a good portion of the summer break working part-time as a dishwasher at Naomi-san's restaurant. Jeong-il was working there with me. He was trying to save up to pay for the college admission exams.

"So how've you been doing?" Jeong-il asked with a meaningful smile one day during break period. I hadn't told him about Sakurai yet. But after I'd turned down a couple of his invitations to hang out, he must've sensed something and stopped asking out of consideration to me.

"She's really great," I answered. "I'll introduce her to you soon, I promise."

Jeong-il didn't ask anything more and simply said that he was looking forward to meeting her.

Usually we'd talk about stuff like why black people were able to produce the blues, jazz, hip-hop, and rap, but Zainichi couldn't create their own unique culture. But on this day, we talked about mindless trash—like whether we would die for Kim Basinger, whether Ringo would be the obvious choice if we had to fire one of the Beatles, and whether Superman's piston action would be really super—and laughed our heads off.

Toward the end of our break, Jeong-il stopped laughing and asked, as if he'd just remembered, "Do you remember the 'Test of Courage'?"

"What are you talking about?"

"Crazy, you really were something else," said Jeong-il, narrowing his eyes at me.

"But you weren't there at the platform, were you?"

Jeong-il shook his head. "I was there, away from where you and your group were, and I saw you."

The "Test of Courage" was a test of nerves that was passed down as tradition in my junior high school. I called it the "Super Great Chicken Race."

The game was very simple: stand at the edge of the train platform, jump down onto the tracks when the train was fifty meters away from pulling into the platform, and run down the track from one edge of the platform to the other. The story was you were supposed to be able to outrun the train without getting killed if you ran a 12-second 100-meter dash, but since it's likely someone at my school made that calculation, the story lacked credibility. Whatever the case, if you tripped, you were history. If you got freaked and stopped midway, you were history.

If you were too slow and let the train catch you, you were history. If you escaped underneath the platform or to the adjacent track, you were given the title of Queen and were treated as everyone's errand boy, so you were pretty much history anyway. In short, if you were going to do the challenge, you had no choice but to succeed.

Given the severity of the rules, few challengers stepped forward, and only two people had ever succeeded before I came along. One was a senpai about twelve years my senior, who later became a "bullet"—a hit man for the yakuza, who was sent into action because he was expendable—and died. The other was Tawake.

I decided to take the challenge to commemorate my citizenship changing from North Korean to South Korean. At the time, I was able to run 100 meters somewhere in the 11-second range, so I was confident that I would succeed. In the end, I came out of it with flying colors, but because I had tried at all, everyone started to believe that I really was crazy. The two senpai who'd succeeded before me had deliberately dropped a 10,000-yen bill on the track, creating a situation of having to retrieve it in order to psych themselves up. I had simply hopped down on the track and outran the train without dropping anything.

After some hesitation, I decided to tell Jeong-il the secret to my success. The trick was that I had secretly invited a girl I liked to the train station to watch. The plan, of course, was for her to witness my brave act and fall head over heels for me. But that plan failed spectacularly. The girl didn't have a clue how men's minds worked.

She said, "Maybe you should get your head examined at the hospital."

Jeong-il cackled with pure delight at my story. After a while, he composed himself and said, "If I were a girl, I'd fall for you."

I said, "Right?" and tilted my head.

"You were really something else that day," said Jeong-il, smiling tenderly at me. "For some reason, I remember that image of you running a lot lately. When I'm walking down the street or taking a bath, when I least expect it. I wonder why . . ."

"Maybe you should get your head examined at the hospital."

Jeong-il and I looked at each other and burst out laughing.

On our way back to the kitchen after our break, I said, "We should talk about crap like this more often."

Jeong-il gave me that good-natured smile of his and nodded.

Every moment I could spare from my part-time job, I spent seeing Sakurai. Sakurai had gotten a job as a telephone operator through her father's connections at work. Basically she answered phone calls, which not only was a pretty easy job but paid well, too. Sakurai had kept a savings account since childhood. Add that to what she earned at her job, and she already had quite a sum saved up. I was shocked to hear the amount of money she had when she told me once. She really didn't need to be working that much at all.

During one of our dates, Sakurai said, "Let's take the mock exams together."

She took out a blank application form from a famous cram school for a mock college entrance exam and handed it to me.

"You're planning to go to university, right?" she asked.

I nodded slightly.

"Then you should definitely take it as practice."

As she said this, Sakurai looked longingly at me. How could I refuse? I nodded. She smiled. And so, on a Sunday toward the end of August, I went with Sakurai and took the mock exams for the first time. The results would be announced about a month later.

One night toward the end of summer vacation, I got a phone call from Kato.

"I've got a great gig for you."

It was a job as a bouncer at a dance party Kato was organizing.

Hosting dance parties was a thing at my high school. It was an easy way to get girls and earn a nice profit from ticket sales. But amateurs that tried to get in on the action got hurt. There were more than a few flies buzzing around that sweet deal. Naturally, a war over profits ensued. A fly that didn't have muscle was easily squashed. Battles with organizers from other schools over ticket sales and customers were always raging. Things would sometimes get violent, and those battles ended with a ride down to the police station. The party organizer would see his cred go down and customers disappear when that happened, so he tried to avoid trouble when he could. That's when bouncers were necessary; the more there were, the less chance of enemies crashing the party. But to my knowledge, none of Kato's dance parties had ever suffered an enemy attack. Anyone that dared to crash one of Kato's dance parties without fear of his old man had to be one crazy bastard.

"Some guys get drunk and get out of hand," said Kato. "I'm asking you to bounce them out when that happens."

Kato had a number of henchmen working for him. He certainly didn't need me in that role. I asked him how much he was paying. It was roughly the amount I earned in a month washing dishes at Naomi-san's restaurant. Kato knew that I was trying to save up for Sakurai.

"You sure?" I asked.

"Come on, don't be a pain."

"I owe you one."

"Sure, see you next Saturday."

Saturday night I headed for Z, the club where Kato had his birthday party. I entered the club and, just as the last time, was greeted by the pulse of electronica, cigarette smoke, the smell of alcohol, and body heat, along with the sight of Takeshita taking tickets. Takeshita pointed to the table I'd sat at before. Every table in the club was full except for that one. I gave Takeshita a pat on the back and made my way to the table.

I sat down. Since I didn't have anything to do, I opened up the paperback I'd brought and began reading by the flame of the spirit lamp on the table. It was *In Exile*, the book I'd borrowed from Jeong-il a while back. Things had been so hectic that I'd hardly touched it since Jeong-il lent it to me.

Two glasses filled with iced oolong tea appeared on the table. I looked up and found Kato. I was so focused on the book that I hadn't noticed him. I closed the book at the same time Kato sat down across from me.

"Sorry I'm not a snow spirit," he said, making a reference to the night I'd met Sakurai.

Kato and I exchanged a look and laughed.

"You guys getting along?"

I nodded. "Yeah," I muttered.

After taking a sip from his glass, Kato asked, "Does the snow spirit know about you?"

"How do you mean?"

"I mean, does she know everything about you?"

"I'm thinking about telling her . . . soon."

Scratching his head, Kato said, "Probably none of my business anyway," and drank the rest of his tea. Then he asked, "What're you planning on doing after high school?"

"I haven't really decided yet," I answered.

"Then why don't we team up and expand our turf?"

"Expand? Just what are you thinking about doing?"

Kato leaned slightly out of his seat. "I'm going to manage a club. It's going to be off the hook. One of those cutting-edge clubs where all the celebrities hang out. Why don't we do it together?"

"If you're looking for a bouncer, you'd be better off with some has-been solider from one of the American military bases."

He shook his head with irritation. "I'm not making you a bouncer. We're going to be comanagers."

"I don't have any money."

"Money?" he spat out. "My father will give us all the money we need. I just want to keep you close is all."

"You're not gay, are you?" I joked, trying to get Kato to slow down. "Hardcore?"

Kato didn't even crack a smile. "People like you and me have been handicapped our whole lives. We're like twins. If people like us are going to get anywhere in this country, we can't just walk in through the front door. You get that, don't you? We can lay low in the shadows and make it big and stick it to all the uppity miserable bastards that ever discriminated against us. Because *we* can do that. Because we're meant for greatness."

I stared at the beads of sweat on the outside of the glass and said nothing. Kato's body twitched as if to prompt an answer.

Raising my eyes from the glass, I said, "You and I are nothing alike. We're different."

A deep frown line creased his forehead. Kato opened his mouth to protest when—

"Stop!"

There was the high-pitched cry of a girl from the dance floor below. Kato choked back what he was about to say and left his seat. As his resident bouncer, I got up and looked down on the floor from the railing.

There was a guy and girl tussling in the middle of the dance floor. The guy looked familiar. He looked like a kid—Kobayashi—in the same year as me at school. The rumor had been that the poser was talking trash behind my back about kicking my ass.

Kobayashi had grabbed the girl by the elbow and was pulling her toward him. The girl cried, "Stop!" again and slapped him hard across the face. With the sound of the slap, almost everyone stopped dancing and began to move away, as if on cue. The DJ stopped the music.

Realizing all eyes were trained on him, Kobayashi was faced with having to choose between one of two moves. Naturally, he made the wrong one. The sound of his palm connecting with the girl's face echoed across the floor. Pressing a hand against her cheek, the girl shouted, "Scumbag!" As Kobayashi's hand went into motion again, Kato's voice rained down from above. "Hey!" Kobayashi stopped and turned his eyes up at Kato and me. Slowly he lowered his hand. But his eyes were bloodshot, and he looked as if he might come after us at any moment. Kato looked down at him with a sneer smeared across his lips. That was a mistake. Unable to back down amid the stares of the crowd, Kobayashi made another bad move.

"Think you're pretty big with that damn Chon next to you?"

Chon. The nasty Japanese word for a Korean had a familiar ring to it. It was an epithet that I'd had hurled at me at least fifty times, from as far back as I could remember. And I'd responded to it with my fists at least fifty times.

Kato looked at me. I shrugged. Kato made like he was going down-stairs, so I grabbed him by the arm and stopped him. Again Kobayashi shouted from below.

"Come on down, Chon-boy! Or maybe you'd like to go back to your country with your tail between your legs!"

A shadow came over Kato's eyes. I let go of his arm and said, "See what I mean? We're different."

Leaving Kato standing on the loft, I went down the stairs to the dance floor. The entire club was heated with a tension that could burn your skin. I closed the distance between Kobayashi and me until we were a yard apart. His face was twisted into an ambiguous expression.

It wasn't clear whether he was crying or laughing. I stared at the strange look on his face and said, "Do you know the meaning of the country name Japan?"

For an instant, the strangeness of the question broke the tension in his face. I drilled him in the face dead center with a straight punch, a good right. Kobayashi let out a grunt, covered his nose, and sank to the floor. I looked down at him and waited to finish him off.

After removing his hand from his nose and seeing the blood on his palm, Kobayashi reached into his pants pocket and pulled out something metallic. *Shwing shwing shwing shwing*—it unfolded into a butterfly knife in Kobayashi's hand. The crowd gulped in horror. Kobayashi slowly got to his feet.

I had no intention of entertaining the crowd with a show, so I landed a right toe kick in the groin, where he was completely defenseless. There was drool coming out of his mouth as Kobayashi doubled over on the floor again. Bringing my foot back down, I circled behind him and pushed the back of his head with my foot. Kobayashi slowly tilted forward until he lay flat, spread out on the floor like a pinned frog waiting to be dissected.

Kobayashi was still gripping his precious butterfly knife. I brought my foot down on his wrist. The knife came out of his hand. After picking it up, I put one foot on the base of his head—the medulla—and put my weight on it. If he struggled too hard, his spine would snap.

I said, "If you bring a knife to a fight, you're asking to get cut by one."

What the hell am I saying?

The lower half of Kobayashi's body began to tremble.

"Besides, I could stab you with this knife, and it would be self-defense. You were the one that pulled a knife on me. I have plenty of witnesses."

I took a look around. Not a single person would look me in the eye.

What the hell am I doing here?

"I should stab you in the stomach, but I'll let you off easy this time. I either slice off both your ears or cut off your thumbs. You choose. Put up one finger if you say ears, two fingers for the thumbs."

This isn't what I want to say at all.

Kobayashi balled his hands into fists, refusing to answer. His whole body was twitching almost imperceptibly.

"Both, then." I started to move, and Kobayashi let out a girlish scream, causing a chain reaction of cries from the girls in the crowd.

"Let him go," a voice called out from behind. I turned around and saw Kato.

"Let him go," he said again.

Kato and I silently looked each other in the eye. I folded up the knife, and after tossing it to Kato, I took my foot off the base of Kobayashi's head. I walked past Kato, went up the stairs to the loft, grabbed the copy of *In Exile* I'd left on the table, and headed for the door. Every eye in the club was focused on me. Kato and Takeshita were standing side by side at the door. Takeshita looked down, avoiding eye contact with me. Kato took out a wad of bills from his pants pocket.

Taking my eyes off the money, I looked at Kato. He looked like he was about to cry any second.

"I'm sorry," he said.

I gave Kato a gentle pat on the back, opened the door, and went out. A muggy summer wind blew in my face. The moon was hidden behind thick clouds. I started walking in the direction of Tokyo Tower.

Despite taking several wrong turns along the way, I managed to find the elementary school from that night with Sakurai. As I stood in a daze in front of the iron gate that Sakurai had straddled so proudly, it began to rain. Leaning up against the gate, I let the rain hit me for a while. I recalled the last training session I had with my father.

"I wonder if heaven really is a good place . . ."

I thought of jumping up and down like my father did that night but decided against it. The rain coming down was pathetic. It was barely a drizzle. I prayed for it to rain harder, but it was no good. The rain was already beginning to let up.

Why didn't I jump then, with my father, when I had the chance?

Summer vacation ended, and the second semester began.

I had saved up just enough to go to Okinawa, so Sakurai and I decided to go to the beaches there. Now it was all just a matter of when. We decided to carefully devise a plan.

Kato stopped turning up. In fact, he didn't seem to be coming to school at all. I figured he was on another trip and didn't think much of it.

The results of the mock exams came back. To my surprise, my academic rating went up from about the calories of an egg white to that of egg custard. Reading all those dense books might have helped. After seeing my scores, Sakurai turned glum and said, "That's great," several times. She didn't show me her scores.

"Let's get out of here," she said, with a depressed look on her face.

We left the fast-food restaurant that was near the cram school. Sakurai's feet pointed not in the direction of the nearest train station but in a different direction.

"Let's walk a little to the next station."

I nodded and fell in line next to her. For a while, we walked in silence. Sakurai did all the things that a child might do, like kick at the stones on the pavement and touch every one of the telephone poles along the street.

We walked for about fifteen minutes and came to a bus stop with a bench.

"Let's sit down," Sakurai said.

We took a seat on the bench.

"So what's going on?" I asked.

Sakurai let out a breath and said, "I feel so stupid. I mean really lame."

I waited in silence for her to continue.

"My scores were worse than the last time. I tend to get pretty depressed about stuff like this. Even knowing how colossally silly it is, I can't help it."

"I don't think it's silly," I said.

"Really?" said Sakurai. "You don't think I'm being lame for getting depressed over some test scores?"

"You took the test seriously, right?"

"Yes."

"Then there's nothing wrong with getting depressed. I'd say that's natural."

"Why?"

"If someone took the test, didn't get the scores they wanted, and was laughing about it like they didn't give a damn, that would be lame. Whether it's a test or the 100-meter dash in the Olympics—I don't think it's any different."

Sakurai looked me in the eyes and asked, "Do you really think so?"

"A hundred percent."

A relieved look came over her face.

"Do you ever get depressed, Sugihara?"

I nodded. "Of course I do."

"About what, for example?"

"About a lot of things."

Leaning forward, Sakurai peered up at my eyes. "If you're depressed, I hope you'll talk to me about it."

I nodded.

Sakurai was in high spirits the rest of the way to the station and kept body-checking me.

"Do you know what my sister said?" Sakurai asked, while landing a roundhouse kick to my thigh. "She said you were very good looking. Especially the way your eyes are so sharp and intense. She said you're like a classic Japanese man."

Spotting a plastic frog on display outside a pharmacy, Sakurai cheered and ran toward it. Gazing at her from behind, I went back and forth over whether I should tell her everything about me. But the instant I saw her slamming a roundhouse kick into the frog's body, nothing seemed to matter. I ran over next to her and drilled the frog in the head with a roundhouse kick. A man who might've been the manager came out of the pharmacy, yelling, "What do you think you're doing?!" so we took off down the street. Sakurai grabbed my hand as we ran. I squeezed her hand firmly in mine. We ran with all our might.

By all appearances, everything was going great.

One Tuesday the first week into October, I received a call from Jeong-il. A quiet rain was falling that night.

"How about we meet on Sunday?" he said excitedly.

"I've got plans that day."

Jeong-il persisted. "Come on, just for a little while."

"Is it something you can tell me over the phone?"

"No, I want to tell you face-to-face."

"What's this about?"

"Something really awesome."

"Awesome how?"

"Listen, it's something I really want to tell you about, something only you'd understand."

I conjured up my schedule for that day in my head and said, "How about after noon?"

"What time?"

"Between one and three."

"Perfect."

"Same place as usual?"

"One o'clock at the east exit of Shinjuku Station."

"Okay. Come on, just give me a clue."

"See you Sunday."

He hung up.

5

There was a seventeen-year-old boy who went to high school in Tokyo.

He fell in love with a girl that he always saw on the train platform on his way to school. It was love at first sight. She was also a student at a high school in Tokyo and was very pretty.

Every time he saw her, his heart ached terribly. He didn't know how to tell her what he was feeling. To begin with, he had no idea what language to use to speak to a girl like her. None of the adults in his life had taught him about such things, nor had he been taught much about people of her kind. She wore a *chima geogori*, the traditional girls' uniform of North Korean schools.

After some hesitation, the boy confided in his friends. Naturally they teased him and goaded him on, saying, "We'll be standing right next to you when you tell her." The boy didn't have it in him to protest. He was a shy and delicate boy. One of his friends said, "Keep this to psych yourself up," and gave him a butterfly knife.

One Wednesday morning, the boy and his friends gathered on the platform. She appeared before them at the same time she usually arrived. The girl's beauty took the boys' breath away. A passenger nearby overheard one of the boys say, perhaps out of jealousy: "If you get turned down by a Korean girl, you have to be our errand boy."

Goaded on by his friends, the boy timidly approached the girl. He stood diagonally behind her.

"Um . . ."

The girl trembled reflexively. North Korean terrorism, suspicions of abductions of Japanese citizens, and the nuclear program were burdens the girl wearing the chima geogori was made to bear on her slender shoulders. Once she'd been punched in the shoulder by a fiftyish salary-man. On this very platform.

Fearfully she turned around and caught sight of the boy blinking nervously before her. He looked familiar. He'd been on the same train car several times and had glared at her with a terrifying look.

Holding her bag up to her chest, she unconsciously braced herself and asked, "What is it?"

What must he have been feeling just then?

Intimidated by the overwhelming beauty of her voice? Or shocked by the realization that she could speak Japanese? He just stared at her face, saying nothing. Shrinking under his gaze, threatened, she looked all around her, crying for help inside. The surrounding passengers quickly averted their eyes, so as not to get caught looking.

A student came up the stairs and emerged onto the platform. As if it were the most natural thing in the world, he met her gaze and heard her silent cries for help. He was her senpai. He despised North Korea for making his *kohai* suffer in this way, despised the misguided Japanese who bullied the weak. He quickly went up to the boy and shoved him in the back. I couldn't bring myself to blame him for his mistake. If I were there, I would've done the same thing. He and I were given to making such assumptions in the circumstances we lived in, always.

The boy stumbled forward, and after righting himself, turned around. A male student in a school blazer was standing there, staring at him with a serious look.

For a second, they stared each other down, quiet. According to the stories in the papers, the boy later told the police that he believed that the other guy was the girl's boyfriend and was out to hurt him. He was scared. He had felt ashamed and embarrassed because everyone was looking at him. He couldn't remember what happened next.

An announcement that a train was arriving came over the PA. As if it were some kind of cue, the boy pulled out a butterfly knife from his jacket pocket, clumsily unfolded the knife, and pointed it toward the student's chest. The student had never been in a fistfight before, and, obviously, never had a knife pointed at him before. Even when I—a seasoned brawler—had a knife pulled on me for the first time, I felt all the pores on my body open up in an instant and almost peed in my pants.

The student—Jeong-il—was braver than I was. Without flinching, he edged closer to the boy to try to knock the knife out of his hand with his bag. I should've told him that when I had a knife pulled on me for the first time, I ran faster than Carl Lewis. That the only people who survive in this world are cowards. And that true heroes are destined to die young. That the world needed him, so if anyone pulled a knife on him, he had to run faster than a speeding bullet.

As he stepped forward, Jeong-il raised his bag up over his head and swung down with all his might. The boy threw his free hand up in front of his face and took the hit. The distance between them closed. When Jeong-il raised the bag again, the terrified boy reflexively swung the knife upward in a diagonal motion. It happened at the same moment Jeong-il leaned in as he swung his bag again.

The knife plunged into the carotid artery running down the left side of Jeong-il's neck. The boy pulled back the knife as if to shake off the horrible sensation running up his arm, and Jeong-il's bag came down on the knife. The knife clattered as it hit the ground. The train pulled into the platform. Jeong-il instinctively pressed his palm up against where the knife had been. Blood began to spray out like a shower from between his fingers.

Having seen everything up close from beginning to end, the girl opened her eyes wide, parted her lips slightly, and let out a silent scream.

In the blink of an eye, and I truly mean in the time it takes to blink, the white shirt beneath Jeong-il's blazer seeped with dark blood. Seeing the blood, the boy pitched forward and began to throw up everything in his stomach. Jeong-il fell to his knees on the platform. The girl put her tiny hands over Jeong-il's hand, covering the carotid artery. In an instant, her hands were soaked in blood. The train came to a stop and opened its doors. Not a single passenger boarded the train from the door nearest Jeong-il, the girl, and the boy.

"Please call an ambulance!" cried the girl to no one in particular.

Turning a deaf ear to the girl's plea, passengers filed into the train in an orderly fashion.

Again the girl cried toward the many doors sliding closed, "Please call an ambulance!"

As if nothing had happened, the train pulled out of the platform and headed for the next station. The friends who had goaded the boy on had disappeared.

Finally, a young station attendant appeared. "Is anything the matter?"

"Please call an ambulance!"

The attendant, reacting to the desperation of her cry, rushed immediately to the stationmaster's office. Jeong-il's limp body slumped against the girl. She caught him. She sat down on the floor, holding him in her arms from behind, and rested his body on her lap. There was nothing more she could do for him. From the time the ambulance arrived to when the gurney was finally brought over, she glared, first at the boy still vomiting in front of her and then at the curious onlookers ogling from afar. When the paramedics finally came with the gurney, she cried inconsolably, large tears falling down her cheeks.

Jeong-il bled out. By the time the ambulance got to the hospital, it was already too late. The police arrested the boy. Due to his diminished mental state, the interrogation was cut short, and he was sent to a detention house. The boy suffered from a severe case of diarrhea in the middle of the night and became dehydrated. He was taken out of detention and sent to a university hospital nearby. Hospital staff was preparing the boy's IV in a room on the sixth floor, with its large window half open. Apparently, it happened very quickly. The boy, who until then had been lying in bed, unable to walk, suddenly rushed to the window, slid it all the way open, and put one foot on the windowsill. He stopped and turned around, and after muttering "sorry" in the general direction of the staff in the room, climbed over the windowsill and threw himself into the darkness. The boy and Jeong-il died on the same day. The hospital was also the same hospital Jeong-il had been taken to.

It was a tragedy. There was no two ways about it. But whatever the tragedy, people are desperate to find even a fragment of salvation. I was no different. Two days after the incident, I talked to an old friend from my Korean school days, and he gave me an account of the girl on the platform:

Jeong-il lay slumped in the girl's lap when suddenly his head moved. There was a faint smile on his pale face. His gaze was directed at the track, his eyes slowly moving as if he were watching a train pull into the platform.

Jeong-il had been watching me run down the track. I was sure of it. I wanted it to be true. And what was the problem if it was?

The night of the incident, I learned about Jeong-il's death through a phone call from his mother. Not even twenty-four hours had passed since Jeong-il's call the night before.

"Jeong-il has died," Jeong-il's mother said as soon as I answered the phone. Her voice sounded clearer than usual and very beautiful.

I wasn't fully able to grasp the meaning of the words and could only utter, "Huh?" And as if my voice was some kind of cue, she began to cry. Her feeble sobs trickled into my ears. I restrained myself from asking too many questions and listened to Jeong-il's mother sobbing. The phone beeped several times, signaling a call on the other line. I ignored the call, silently cursing whoever it was that invented call waiting.

After crying for nearly twenty minutes, Jeong-il's mother apologized and explained what had happened.

"Jeong-il adored you, Sugihara-kun. Thank you for being his friend," she said before hanging up the phone.

I only answered, "Yes."

After hanging up the phone, I lay on my bed and stared at the ceiling. I must've stared for about an hour. But what I'd been thinking about I can't remember.

I got up and went into the living room. My mother was gone, away on a trip with Naomi-san in Phuket. My father was watching an instructional video on golf.

"Jeong-il's dead."

My father pressed stop on the remote control and turned off the TV. I told him what had happened. After listening to my story, he muttered, "I see," and let out a deep sigh. Then he got up off the sofa, came up to me, and roughing up my hair, said, "Try not to think too hard about it. For now, it's best you cry your eyes out and eat whatever the hell you want."

I nodded. I said thanks and left. A few minutes after I returned to my room, the phone rang. I pressed the button on the handset, and it was Sakurai on the line.

"You didn't pick up earlier," she said.

I wavered over telling her about Jeong-il, but in the end, I decided against it. I didn't have the energy or confidence to clearly explain to her everything that had happened.

"I just have a lot going on right now," I said. "Can I call you tomorrow?"

After a brief silence, Sakurai asked, "Did something happen?"

"I'll tell you about it soon, I promise."

"Okay . . . so I guess I'll talk to you tomorrow."

As I moved to hang up the phone, Sakurai hastily said, as if she had just remembered, "You remember our date on Sunday, right?"

"Yeah."

"Oh, good."

I hung up the phone.

Sunday morning, I left the house.

Soon after Sakurai and I started dating, we'd promised to go to the opera together as part of our hunt for "cool" stuff. Neither of us had seen an opera before.

We had been listening to famous operas on CD and picking out the ones we might like to actually see. *The Marriage of Figaro*, *Tannhäuser*, *Madama Butterfly*, *The Knight of the Rose*, *Cavalleria rusticana*, *La traviata* . . .

I said that I wanted to see *Cavalleria rusticana*, and Sakurai said that she really wanted to see *La traviata*. Naturally I was the one to cave. We agreed to go see *La traviata*, but unfortunately there were no performances in the near future. Sakurai was planning to spend several months, starting in November, studying for the entrance exams, so we only had until October. Then we discovered *Cavalleria rusticana* was going to be playing in the middle of October.

We bought the tickets for a shocking amount of money in the beginning of August and began studying up on the opera. We learned the lyrics and storyline by listening to the CD countless times in the media room. We steadily carried out preparations for attending our first opera.

Everything was set. So when I called Sakurai and canceled on Saturday, the night before the performance, she sounded pretty upset.

"Why?"

"I have to go to a funeral for a friend."

She fell silent for a moment and then asked, "When did your friend die?"

"Wednesday."

"Why didn't you tell me until today?"

I couldn't answer.

"That's messed up, definitely."

"You're right."

For a while there was a heavy silence between us.

"Was he an old friend?" asked Sakurai.

"Yeah."

"Is it that I'm not reliable or something?"

"Why do you think that?"

"If I had an old friend die, I would definitely tell you about it and ask you to help me through it. Besides, didn't I tell you to talk to me if you're ever depressed?"

"I'm sorry. But this doesn't have anything to do with you being reliable or not. Really. I'll tell you about it soon. I promise."

Sakurai said nothing more to try to make me feel guilty. I asked her to go with someone else so the ticket wouldn't go to waste, and she answered disappointedly, "Maybe I will."

Since I overshot my intended train station by two stops and the bus stop by three, I was nearly an hour late to the funeral.

When I went inside the enormous hall not too far from Jeong-il's house, the funeral had already come to the climax, and Jeong-il's uncle on his mother's side was giving a speech. Despite wondering why Jeong-il's mother wasn't giving the speech, I shook it off and in a daze stared at Jeong-il's mother holding a framed portrait of Jeong-il in her arms as the uncle droned on. She looked terribly worn out.

During the ten minutes I listened to his speech, the uncle must've said, "Jeong-il didn't live to see his twentieth birthday" three times. I felt dizzy every time he said it.

The funeral ended. The attendant said, "A light meal has been prepared for everyone, so please make your way to the second floor." I weaved past the others going upstairs and caught up with Jeong-il's mom. We'd only had a chance to exchange silent bows at the wake, so I wanted to give her a proper greeting.

I stood in front of her. She took one look at me, and after letting out a sigh so deep she might deflate into nothing, she began to cry on my chest. The corner of the picture frame containing Jeong-il's portrait hit me several times on the chin.

Jeong-il's mother cried, "Why did he have to die?"

I stood absolutely still and listened as she continued to sob.

A man who might've been an uncle came by and pulled her away from my chest. As I watched her being ushered into the room where Jeong-il would be cremated, someone hit me on the shoulder from behind. When I turned around, a bunch of guys wearing school blazers were standing in front of me. I gave the one I'd assumed had hit me a gentle punch in the stomach. Won-soo jokingly grabbed his stomach with both hands and said with a smile on his rough, square-jawed face, "Long time, no see. You never call."

"You, too."

We smiled at each other somewhat awkwardly.

Won-soo and I had been partners in crime since elementary school. Anytime I was up to no good, he was always by my side. It was Won-soo who hit the cop car with the paint-filled water balloon and who went on the trip to Nagoya with me. And by the way, Won-soo was the one who tailed me, spied me going into a cram school, and then ratted me out to everyone back in the third year of junior high. Since I'd started going to a Japanese high school, we hadn't seen each other once.

"You haven't gone chicken on me, have you?" said Won-soo, drawing his face up to mine. His breath reeked of nicotine. I punched him in the stomach hard this time. Won-soo let out a groan.

"We had a deal."

Won-soo and I made a promise to quit smoking in the summer of our second year in junior high school. The deal was if we caught the other breaking that promise, we were allowed to punch him as punishment, no complaints.

Rubbing his belly with a satisfied smile, Won-soo said, "Why don't we kick up some trouble tomorrow, like the old days?"

"Doing what?"

"We're going on a manhunt."

"For who?"

"The bastard friends of the kid who killed Jeong-il."

"You know who they are?"

"Damn if I know," Won-soo spat out. "I'm sure if we grab someone that goes to the same school and knock them around a little, they'll talk."

Saying nothing, I looked into Won-soo's eyes. Then I looked at the familiar faces of the old friends standing behind me. They looked hungry for a sacrifice.

"Forget it," I said.

"What was that?" A deep line creased his brow.

"What happened to Jeong-il got some attention in the media. You know the police are going to be watching the schools to keep a lid on things."

"So what?" A dark look of violence came over Won-soo's face. "You want us to forget what happened because of the police? Is that it?"

"What do you think is going to happen if you go after those bastards? It's not going to bring—"

Won-soo cut me off midsentence, jabbing his two fingers against my chest. He quickly pulled them back and gave them a curious stare.

His fingers had touched the part of my chest that Jeong-il's mom had been crying on. After wiping the damp tips of his fingers on his blazer, he said, "So are you in or out? Which is it?"

"I'm out," I answered plainly. "And Jeong-il wouldn't want this either."

"Don't bullshit me," said Won-soo in a muted voice. "It's a tragedy what happened to Jeong-il. But he's dead. Gone. Which is why it's up to us, the living, to settle the score that he left behind. And the person Jeong-il wants most to do it is you. But here you are, talking like some kind of chicken."

"Listen to yourself," I answered in a choked voice. "What do you know about Jeong-il? Did any of you even take the time to talk to him? You're only looking to start trouble. In that case, why don't you go mess around with some gangs?"

A terrible air of violence hung over where we stood. Won-soo's glare—shared by the bunch behind me—seemed to stab me until it hurt. I let out a short sigh and said, "Let Jeong-il go in peace."

"What's happened to you?" asked Won-soo with a troubled look. "Did you sell your soul to the Japanese in that school of yours?"

Hearing the word "soul" reminded me of the time Jeong-il recited the passage about the Japanese spirit from *I Am a Cat*. But I couldn't remember how it went. After some thought, I said, "I don't know anything about souls. But if I had something like a North Korean soul, I wouldn't think twice about selling it. You guys want to buy it?"

Won-soo looked at me with a distant gaze.

Come on. Don't look at me like that. Did you forget? You and I didn't have money for a hotel the night we got to Nagoya, so we ended up sleeping in the parking lot next to the pachinko parlor. We lay spread out on the asphalt, looking up at the stars, and talked about going as far away as possible. We can do that, Won-soo. We can go right now . . .

Won-soo jabbed me in the chest again with two fingers.

"I'm finished with you. The next time you see me on the street, keep on walking. If you so much as try to get close to me, I'll jump you."

To the others, he said, "Let's go." They made their way past me. One of them, in passing, whispered contemptuously in my ear, "Traitor. Friendless bat."

After they all walked past me, I turned around only once. Won-soo had stopped and was looking at me. His face was frighteningly expressionless. I forced a smile on my face and directed it at Won-soo. He ignored me and turned his back.

I left the funeral hall. I overshot my intended bus stop by four stops, got on the bus going back in the opposite direction, and then overshot the stop again—by five this time. By the time I got to the train station, it was early evening.

Friendless bat. Going down the stairs to the train platform, for some reason I heard the voice echoing in my ear. *God, I wish I were a bat. I could fly away anywhere,* I thought, when a sudden dizziness came over me, causing me to almost lose my balance. I did an ass-plant in the middle of the stairs. The dizziness quickly went away, but then my chest began to hurt. I let out a low groan. *Ooooo ooooo.*

It was in my second year of junior high school. The basketball team that I played on had advanced to the finals of the national tournament for North Korean schools. Maybe it was because the team we were playing against was from Osaka, but the game took on the atmosphere of a Giants versus Hanshin rivalry game and became strangely heated. Things got so physical on the court that players were hurt; fights even broke out in the stands, causing more injuries. I was playing point guard and took four punches in the face by the kid guarding me. I got him back with a knee kick, elbow, head butt, and finger in the eye. The ref caught me poking the kid in the eye and charged me with a foul.

We lost the game by one point. Afterward, we went into the locker room and hung our heads in silence. Had any one of us started crying, it would likely have infected the whole team in an instant, and we would have all burst into tears. The coach came inside the locker room with the school principal.

"You did a good job. I'm proud of all of you."

Upon hearing these words, one of the first-year players began to cry. Just as everyone's cry button was about to get switched on, the coach went up to the first-year, pulled back his arm like an Olympic discus thrower, and smacked him across the face. The kid went flying and slammed into the lockers with a great big crash! The rest of us shuddered at the sound. In a terribly calm tone, the coach said to no one in particular, "Never cry in front of others. You boys live your lives surrounded by enemies. Shedding tears before the enemy is the same as begging for pity. The same as admitting defeat. Your admitting defeat means all North Koreans are admitting defeat. That's why you can't ever get into the habit of crying in front of others. If you want to cry, go do it alone in the privacy of your room."

The coach glanced over at the principal. The principal gave a slight nod as if nothing had happened.

The coach said, "Now hurry up and get dressed. The principal would like to take you to dinner as a reward for your efforts today."

The coach and principal went out of the locker room. A heavy pall hung over the room. A third-year senpai went over to the first-year who had gotten slapped and patted him on the head. Seeing this, the captain suddenly began to let out a low groan, *Ooooo ooooo*. His eyes were red. The groans quickly became contagious. *Ooooo ooooo*. We all let out groans, our eyes red. We kept on groaning, desperate to keep from crying. Since then, whenever we had something unbearably hard or sad happen to us, letting out this mournful groan—*Ooooo ooooo*—became a secret custom of the basketball team.

And so I sat in the middle of the stairs and groaned. *Ooooo ooooo*. Although the station was teeming with rush-hour commuters, no one came near me. Occasionally, some young salaryman in a suit grumpily clicked his tongue at me. *You guys are my enemies?*

The face of Jeong-il, my steady ally, floated into my head. I gave up groaning and talked to Jeong-il. "So what was that awesome thing you wanted to tell me about? Was it more awesome than mitochondrial DNA? Was it the secret to ridding the world of discrimination—something like that? It really would be awesome if something like that really existed. Hey, you didn't get a girlfriend, did you? I would've liked hearing that better. I mean I've never seen you with a girl. What a waste—you could've gotten any girl you wanted if you'd gone to a Japanese university. There isn't anyone like you. Why did you have to die, Jeong-il? It's going to be pretty tough doing this alone. Why did you have to die?"

I closed my eyes, took a deep breath, and got up off the stairs. I went down the rest of the stairs to the platform and looked for a pay phone. Spotting one next to a kiosk, I started walking. As soon as I grabbed the receiver off the cradle, I realized I'd forgotten my telephone card at home and stuck my hand in my pockets for some change. I couldn't find any ten-yen coins, so I dropped a hundred-yen coin and slowly pushed the numbers for Sakurai's house. Sakurai was supposed to be out at the opera.

We met at a café near Ginza 4-chome.

"I saw this show the other day about how the direct ancestor of modern humans isn't Peking man or Neanderthal man but the australopithecines that originated on the African continent two million years ago. They figured this out by comparing the Neanderthal to modern human mitochondrial DNA sequences—it's all pretty complicated, so I'll explain mitochondrial DNA to you another time. The australopithecines originating in Africa continued to evolve until they came to be the genus *Homo*. Gradually, there were groups that moved out of Africa and spread all over the world. This migration might have been caused by a power struggle, or maybe climate change was the cause.

"When the earth entered the Ice Age roughly 130,000 years ago and Africa became too cold, humans might've set off for warmer places. I actually think we migrated for completely different reasons, but I'll tell you about that later. The humans leaving Africa eventually split into two groups somewhere in the Middle East: one headed for Europe and the other for Asia. This split marked the beginning of the so-called Caucasoid race and us, the Mongoloid race. The group that chose to become the Mongoloid race headed down into Asia, while gradually adapting their body and facial features according to the environment. They never stopped moving their feet. When parents died, their children took over and kept on moving. Then at the end of nearly a hundred thousand years and tens of thousands of miles, a group of Mongoloids found themselves in Japan. This group would later come to be known as the Jomon people and were the ancient inhabitants of Japan. Normally the story would end happily ever after here, but this is where it gets interesting.

"There were some that didn't stop moving even after getting to the Far East. They traveled up the Eurasian continent until they reached Siberia and walked across the Bering land bridge, which was exposed when the sea level dropped during the last ice age, and to the western-most part of the American continent: Alaska. But they weren't satisfied with just crossing to the Americas. They began to move south, down the length of the continent, founding the Mayan and Aztec civilizations along the way. And then they reached the southern edge of South America. It was a journey that took generation after generation to finish, but the courage and glory of those humans who took the first steps remain in the bodies of their descendants. Research proved that these people belonged to the same group as the Mongoloids who stayed in Japan.

"A comparison between the mitochondrial DNA sequences of the Ainu descended from the Jomon people and the indigenous people of the Andes showed them to be basically the same. Isn't that amazing? If you count the distance from Africa, that's a journey of fifteen thousand miles. And you know what? I don't believe that a power struggle or the declining environment was what pushed them to travel all that way. They just had to see what kind of place the edge of the earth was. I'm sure of it. And the genes encoded with this ridiculously simple impulse remained no matter how many generations passed. Besides, humans never had it in them to settle in one place. And then something called agriculture was invented—"

"So what are you trying to say, Sugihara?" asked Sakurai, a gentle smile floating across her lips.

"What I'm trying to say," I said, looking her in the eyes, "is that they're really cool, and I want to be like them."

Her smile grew wider as she said, "You're just trying to impress me, right?"

I nodded earnestly. After letting out a giggle, she peered into my eyes and said, "I saw this show the other day about a retirement home for guide dogs in Hokkaido. It's this place where old dogs that can't do their job anymore can go to live out their last days. The fact that a place like that even existed moved me so much that I couldn't take my eyes off the TV. And then they showed a woman saying goodbye to her guide dog. It was a blind woman and a male golden retriever couple, and she just held him in her arms completely still for a good hour until finally the staff had to pull them apart. As the car drove away from the retirement home, the woman leaned out of the window and waved, shouting, 'See you,' and 'Bye-bye,' and the dog's name, but the dog just sat there and watched the car go. But that's the way it had to be. It's how guide dogs are trained. They aren't allowed to show any excitement, and they aren't allowed to bark. Even after the car was gone, the dog didn't move an inch from where they said their goodbyes, and he kept looking in the direction the car disappeared. For *hours*. The woman who'd been by his side for ten years wasn't there anymore. He must have been so devastated he couldn't move. They said goodbye around noon, and in the evening it started to rain. Really hard. The dog that had been looking straight ahead until then looked up like he was watching the rain come down and started to howl. *Waoon waoon*. Like that—again and again. He didn't look the least bit sad or pathetic. He bayed with his back stretched, and the line from his chest to his chin perfectly straight like a beautiful sculpture. I cried my eyes out. *Waoon waoon*. Just like that."

"So what are you trying to say, Sakurai?" I asked.

"I'm trying to say that I want to love someone the way that dog did. His howl was more beautiful than any music I've ever heard. I want to be the kind of person that can love someone right and then cry the way that dog did if I lost someone. Do you understand what I'm getting at?"

After giving her a firm nod, I reached out and put my hand over Sakurai's on the table. For a while, we looked into each other's eyes and said nothing. The café waiter came by and refilled our water glasses.

Sakurai said, "You've been looking like you're about to cry."

"Really?"

"Yeah."

She looked down, averting her eyes from mine, and let out a breath. Her chest shook slightly.

When I asked, "What's the matter?" she looked up and stared into my eyes.

"Would you like me to be with you tonight?"

"Huh?"

"I can stay with you until you go to sleep and wake up."

"Are you sure?"

"Please don't make me say it again."

We left the café and headed for Yurakucho Station. While Sakurai called home from a pay phone inside the station, I went to put my school uniform jacket in a pay locker nearby. I stood in front of the coin-operated locker and took out two envelopes from my inner pocket. With me arriving late to the funeral and the run-in with Won-soo, I'd forgotten to give Jeong-il's mom my condolence money. First I pulled out 30,000 yen of my own money from one envelope and put it in my pants pocket. Then I opened the envelope my father had given me. He couldn't go to the funeral on account of urgent business. There were ten crisp 10,000-yen bills inside. I put them in my pocket, too. I had a feeling Jeong-il and my father would forgive me.

When I returned to the station, Sakurai was still on the phone. I glanced at the clock on the wall. It was ten minutes to ten.

At exactly ten o'clock, Sakurai finished her call and came running back.

"Any trouble?"

Sakurai hastily shook her head.

"Everything's great. I told my father that I was staying at a friend's house."

We headed for the Imperial Hotel. Since we weren't doing anything wrong, I walked right into the lobby without caring too much about being in shirtsleeves and my school trousers. I parted with Sakurai at the lobby and asked her to wait on the sofa near the tearoom.

I walked up to the front desk. Showing no hint of surprise at the sight of me, the young clerk bowed politely, saying, "Welcome."

"I'd like a room, please," I said.

"Do you have a reservation?"

"No."

And then for the next couple of minutes, he gave me a rundown of the various room types and prices. The prices varied according to what floor the room was on and which way it was facing. After a careful consultation with the clerk, I decided on a deluxe room on the twelfth floor facing Hibiya Park. The view was apparently very nice. The condolence money would more than cover the cost.

"Will you be paying with a credit card or cash?" asked the clerk.

"Cash."

I stuck a hand in my pocket, thinking payment had to be made up front, but the clerk said that the bill would be settled when I checked out. Next, the clerk handed me a guest card, so I began filling it out. To avoid any hassle, I decided to pretend Sakurai and I were married and put down "Sugihara" for both our last names. The problem was with Sakurai's first name, and since it would be weird to go ask her, I decided to give her a random name. So she became "Keiko." I got the room key and walked away.

I found Sakurai, and we boarded the elevator and went up to the twelfth floor. We walked past the floor receptionist, down the long corridor, and stood in front of the door of our room. I opened the door, and we went inside.

When the door closed behind us, Sakurai and I let out a sigh almost at the same time.

"Wow, that was nerve-racking," she said, smiling.

I nodded.

The tastefully decorated hotel room was larger than any I'd ever stayed in. There was a sturdy-looking wood writing desk, a sturdy-looking sofa set, and sturdy-looking picture frames hanging on the walls. Restless, Sakurai and I lost interest in the sturdy-looking furniture and furnishings and went to the bed.

We took off our shoes and hopped up on the double bed, as if it were expected, and jumped up and down like kids. Sakurai nimbly slipped off the red cardigan she was wearing and tossed it toward the wall. Dressed only in a white dress now, she kept on jumping without caring that her panties peeked out from beneath her dress every time she landed. She looked really happy.

After we'd jumped up and down about thirty times and started to lose our breath, Sakurai dove into me. I caught her in midair, and we landed back on the bed together. We stood on the bed, breathless, and stared into each other's eyes. Suddenly, Sakurai planted her lips on mine. We kissed long and hard, our tongues tangling. A couple of times we unlocked lips to come up for air and then went back to kissing again.

I placed my hands on her waist and moved my thumbs up and down, which made her pull her lips away from mine and rest her head on my chest. A breathy gasp escaped her lips. Slowly I ran my hands down her body, grabbed the hem of her dress, and slowly hiked it up. Sakurai raised her arms above her head in a banzai pose. I lifted the dress over her head and tossed it toward the wall.

Stripped down to her underwear and bra now, Sakurai put her hands on the front of my shirt. She undid each button carefully.

I let Sakurai take off my shirt and tank top. She dropped them next to the bed and reached for my belt.

"I'll get out of these myself," I said.

Sakurai chuckled and jumped off the bed. She went to the wall, reached for the light switch and turned off the light. She sat down on the bed and unhooked her bra.

I stepped down from the bed and took off my pants and socks in the dark. I wondered about my boxers but decided to keep them on. When I turned to the bed, I found Sakurai lying on her back. My eyes were getting used to the dark.

Lying down on the bed next to Sakurai, I gently traced the curves of her face with my right thumb. Her forehead, brows, eyes, nose, cheeks, lips. Afterward, I kissed each of those parts gently. Sakurai's breathing was steady and light.

Holding her by the shoulders, I slowly turned her over so she was lying on her stomach. First I ran my tongue over the nape of her neck, occasionally giving her ear lobes a light nip. Sakurai's breathing grew erratic, rough.

Taking my lips off the nape of her neck, I put my left thumb there instead and moved it up and down, right and left. Then I put my lips on the dip of her back and licked it. She tasted more gamy than grassy. My tongue ran down the dip, making her body twitch occasionally. Her midriff heaved up and down every time she took a heavy breath, my head going up and down along with her.

Sakurai's right hand, which was stretched out above her, slowly crept down the bed. Once her hand reached bottom, it moved right and left in search of something. When I brought my free hand closer to hers, she grabbed my hand with surprising force and brought it up toward her face. She turned her head to the side and bit my hand hard. As the sharp pain registered in my brain, my tongue moved faster on her back. I felt Sakurai's breath on the back of my hand.

I removed my tongue from the hollow of her back and propped myself up. I put my hand on her shoulder and rolled Sakurai over on her back. She quit biting my hand and said, "I'm crazy about you."

For an instant, Sakurai's eyes seemed to flash red. I was madly in love with this woman, this luminous body lying before me. I had to tell her. I didn't want to hide anything from her.

I sat up on the bed with my legs folded beneath me.

"What's the matter?" asked Sakurai.

"I'm sorry."

Sakurai let go of my right hand.

I said, "There's something I want you to know."

Propping her elbows against the bed, Sakurai slowly brought herself up to a sitting position.

"Know what?"

"There's something I've been hiding."

"What is it all of a sudden?" Sakurai's voice was filled with worry. "What is it?"

"I . . ."

Seeing me struggling to get out the words, she said half-jokingly, "Do you have a criminal record or something?"

"I've been reprimanded a bunch of times, but no record yet."

"Oh, okay," Sakurai said. "Is it about your family?"

"I can't say that it isn't."

"Does your father have a criminal record?"

"My father can be rough, but he's also righteous."

"Your mother has a record?"

"You're kidding, right?"

"Sugihara," Sakurai said, letting out a sigh. "Can you imagine how awkward this would be if I wasn't kidding just a little?"

"I guess."

"Come on, you can tell me. Then we can go back to what we were doing."

For an instant I considered sweeping it all under the rug by saying, "It's nothing. Now, where were we?" But I was afraid that I might never tell her if I missed this chance. Besides, I believed she would accept anything I told her. And then she would say this: *So what? Now let's go back to what we were doing.*

I took a breath so deep that Sakurai noticed, and I said, "I—I'm not Japanese."

The silence must have gone on for only about ten seconds, but to me it seemed much longer.

"What . . . do you mean?" asked Sakurai.

"My nationality isn't Japanese."

"Then what is it?"

"South Korean."

Sakurai drew her legs, which had been stuck straight out at me, back to her chest and sat with her arms wrapped tightly around them. Her body looked terribly small. I said, "But I was North Korean until the second year of junior high. Three months from now, I may be Japanese. In a year, I may be American. And I may be Norwegian when I die."

"What are you saying?" Sakurai asked in a flat voice.

My heart began to beat faster. "That nationality doesn't mean anything."

Silence. Silence. Silence. Silence.

Finally, Sakurai opened her mouth. "You were born in Japan and raised in Japan?"

I nodded and said, "I grew up breathing pretty much the same air as you did and eating pretty much the same foods you did. But we were educated differently. I went to North Korean school until high school. That's where I learned to speak Korean." After getting out that much, I joked, "I'm actually bilingual. Although I guess in Japan, you only call someone who speaks English bilingual. When I'm watching the Olympics, I can cheer on both Japanese and Korean athletes in their language. Don't you think that's great?"

Sakurai didn't even crack a smile. She was looking at me, emotionless. The silence was terrifying. My heart beat even faster. Faster even than the first time a knife was drawn on me. I searched desperately for something to say. But I was out of luck. A terrible feeling of uneasiness came over me and spread through my entire body, weighing me down. Slowly I stretched my hand out toward her. Sakurai's body flinched. My hand stopped in midair even though my brain was telling it to move. I lowered my hand and asked, "Why?"

Sakurai's mouth opened and closed slightly, as though she were trying to say something. Whatever that something might be, I just wanted to hear her voice. I gently asked her what was wrong to try to coax her.

Lowering her eyes, Sakurai said, "My father . . . since I was little, my father told me that I couldn't go out with Korean or Chinese men."

After I managed to take that in, I asked, "Is there a reason why?"

Sakurai fell silent, so I continued. "Was your father treated badly by a Korean or Chinese person or something? Even if that were the case, I'm not the one who treated your father badly."

"It's not that," Sakurai said weakly.

"Then what?"

"He told me . . . that Korean and Chinese people have tainted blood."

Her words didn't shock me. They were merely words uttered from ignorance and prejudice. It was all too easy to deny such irresponsible words.

I said, "Tell me—what's the distinction? How do you decide he's Japanese or she's Korean or he's Chinese?"

"How . . . ?"

"Is it nationality? Like I said before, you can change your nationality, easily."

"Where they were born . . . or the language they speak . . ."

"Then what about returnee kids, born and raised in another country because of their parents' work, who have citizenship in another country. Are they not Japanese?"

"I guess if their parents are Japanese, they're Japanese, too."

"So basically who you are has to do with your roots. Then maybe I should ask how far you have to go back to know your roots. If you found out that your great-grandfather had Chinese blood in him, would you stop being Japanese?"

Sakurai didn't speak.

"Or are you Japanese anyway? Because you were born and raised in Japan, and you speak Japanese? Then that would mean I'm Japanese, too."

"It isn't possible my great-grandfather had Chinese blood," she said with a hint of displeasure in her voice.

"You're wrong," I said a bit firmly. "Your family name, 'Sakurai,' was a name given to people who originally came from China. It's all in the *New Selection and Record of Hereditary Titles and Family Names* compiled during the Heian period."

"I thought that in the past, people didn't have family names, and they randomly gave them to themselves. So there's no way to tell if my ancestors were Chinese at all."

"Exactly. It's also possible that one of your ancestors was adopted into the Sakurai family. Then let's go back further. Your family can't drink alcohol, right?"

Sakurai nodded slightly.

I continued. "The Jomon people are believed to be the direct ancestors of modern Japanese, and there wasn't a single person among them that couldn't drink alcohol. That was proven by DNA research. In fact, all Mongoloids were capable of drinking in ancient times. But then, about twenty-five thousand years ago, a human with a gene mutation was born in Northern China. That human was born with a low tolerance for alcohol. At some point, that person's descendants came to Japan and spread the low-tolerance-for-alcohol gene. And you've inherited that gene. Does that mean your blood containing this Chinese-born gene is tainted?"

Silence.

I sat motionless and waited for Sakurai to speak.

Finally, she let out a long, long breath and said, "You know so much about so many things. But this isn't about any of that. I get what you're trying to say intellectually, but I can't. I'm scared. When I think about you entering my body, I'm scared."

My heart gradually went back down to its normal beat, and the uneasiness weighing me down began to fade at the same time. I let out a much, much longer breath than Sakurai's.

I turned my back to her and climbed off the bed. I picked up the white tank top, which stood out in the darkness, and put it on.

Sakurai said, "Why did you keep this from me for this long? If you didn't think it was such a big deal, you could've told me."

I picked up my shirt and slipped my arms through the sleeves. Then I buttoned up the front.

Sakurai continued. "It's not fair . . . the way you just dropped this on me and ruined everything."

I looked for my socks, thinking to put them on before my pants, but I couldn't find them. I crouched down and combed the floor with my hands. They were nowhere to be found.

Seeing my confusion, Sakurai said, "They're probably in the legs of your pants."

I grabbed my pants and stuck my hand in the legs. There they were.

Sakurai said, "Boys usually panic and rush to take off their pants and socks at the same time. That's why they usually get lost in there."

I sat on the floor and put on my socks. When I finished getting on one sock, she said, "That phone call earlier? That was my sister. When I told her that we were spending the night, she told me about the socks. So I could tell you if you couldn't find your socks. She said that if I did that, that would keep me in the driver's seat in our relationship. And that if a girl didn't act confident on her first night of sex, the guy might walk all over her."

I finished putting on my other sock. I grabbed my pants and got to my feet. When I put one leg into the pants, Sakurai said, "This was going to be my first time. Even if it wasn't, I still would have been scared."

I finished zipping up my pants. I took the room key out of my pants pocket and left it on the side table next to the bed. Sakurai said, "Please say something."

As I walked toward the door, Sakurai said toward my back, "My given name is Tsubaki. Like Tsubaki from *La traviata*. A name that has the kanji characters for cherry blossom and camellia sounds so Japanese that I didn't want you to know."

I put my hand on the doorknob. After wavering a bit, I turned around and said, "My real name is Lee. Like Bruce Lee. My name sounds so foreign that I didn't want you to know because I was afraid of losing you—like I just did."

I opened the door and went out into the corridor. As I slipped out the door, Sakurai seemed to say something, but I couldn't make out what.

When I went back to the front desk, the young clerk seemed a bit wary about my sudden reappearance. I settled the bill and informed him that I would be the only one checking out. I expected his suspicion to grow stronger, but it didn't. The clerk was probably very well trained.

"How did you find the view?" he asked, after I'd paid the bill. I'd actually forgotten to take a look at the magnificent view. I lied and said it was fabulous. The clerk thanked me, smiled politely, and bowed.

Although the trains were still running, I decided to walk home.

I walked on a street parallel with the JR tracks and headed for Tokyo. When I reached Tokyo Station, I realized that I'd left my school uniform jacket in the locker. It was a chilly October night.

I went past Tokyo Station and continued along the tracks toward Kanda. I went inside the convenience store in front of Kanda Station and bought myself a pack of Short Hopes and a cheap lighter. The young cashier took one look at me and opened his mouth to say something but gave up when I glared at him. He handed me the cigarettes.

It was the first cigarette I'd smoked in four years. I coughed at first, but soon found my old groove and smoked the whole pack by the time I got to Ueno. The first convenience store I tried refused to sell me another pack, but the second store did not. I bought two packs just in case.

Smoking my cigarettes, humming a tune, and walking across the guardrail like it was a high wire, I continued moving at a good clip. By the time I reached Nishi-Nippori Station, it was past three in the morning. My house wasn't too much farther. Sometime after four, I was back near my neighborhood of Hakusan. As I walked down the deserted residential street, I spotted a bike with its light on coming toward me. I let out a deep sigh. From the speed at which it was approaching, I instantly recognized the breed of human behind the wheel. I had a truly long relationship with these guys. In *The Long Goodbye*, Philip Marlowe said this about cops: "No way has yet been invented to say goodbye to them."

I wondered what to do with the cigarettes and lighter. Once in my first year of junior high, I was questioned by the police and had my belongings searched. Thanks to a pack of matches, I nearly was framed for being a serial arsonist who was going around starting fires at the time.

The cop had asked, "What are you doing with these matches?"

And I came up with a quip that Ikkyu-san might say: "I'm in charge of keeping the stove warm."

Well, that seemed to sour the cop's mood and got me hauled down to the station and nearly framed for arson.

I thought of ditching the cigarettes and lighter on the side of the street, but I stayed put, not wanting to arouse suspicion. The bicycle sped up a bit and made a beeline for me. At times the bike light shone directly in my eyes and blinded me.

"Hey, what are you doing here at this hour?" asked the cop, climbing off the bicycle. His face was clouded with a dark look of suspicion and the cold-bloodedness of a predator eying his prey. Anticipating what might come next, I casually shifted position so the cop had to stand in front of his parked bike.

"I was out with some friends and missed the last train, so I'm walking back home." I gave him a straight answer.

"Where are you coming from?"

When I told him Yurakucho, the young cop said, "That's far," and nodded as though he appreciated my efforts. Normally the conversation would end here with, "Be careful getting home," but the guy was a pro. Maybe he'd gotten a scent of my junior high school days.

"Where do you live?" he asked with a stern face. It was another textbook question.

Now let's say I gave him my address. The young cop would get on the radio and have someone at the station check the resident register. At that point, it would come out that I'm Zainichi Korean. The young cop would be so informed. Then he would ask, "Do you have your alien registration card?" Japan used to have a law called the Alien Registration Law, which oversaw the foreigners living in Japan. Although "oversaw" had a nice ring to it, the law was basically there to put a collar on so-called "bad" foreigners. Despite being born and raised in Japan, I was still considered a foreign resident, so I was required to be registered as one and have an alien registration card. You were supposed to have this card on your person at all times and not having it could get you a year of penal labor or imprisonment or a fine of 200,000 yen. Anyone who took off his collar would get disciplined. Since I wasn't some farm animal kept by the state, I refused to wear my collar. And I wasn't about to start now.

So anyway, I was standing in front of this young cop in full violation of the law.

"Well? Why don't you answer?" the cop coaxed in a disagreeable tone.

This was long past getting irritating, annoying, and tiresome. Philip Marlowe would have had a snappy comeback and talked his way out of this scrape, but I was no Philip Marlowe. So I decided to hit and run.

In one efficient motion, I thrust out the palm of my hand and hit him in the Adam's apple. The cop let out a choked gasp, stumbling backward. With the bicycle parked right behind him, he wasn't able to get his balance, and he fell backward on the bike saddle. Unable to support his weight, the bike toppled sideways, carrying the cop with it.

Just as I had planned. As soon as the cop stumbled, I took off running. The plan was to run out of sight before the cop had a chance to recover and chase me. I was confident that I could. I was used to police chases.

Behind me, I heard an unexpected sound. Thud! Slowing down, I turned around to see the young cop sprawled out on top of the fallen bike, completely still. His police cap had come off, leaving his bare head exposed. I slowed to a stop. He didn't look like he was faking. My sighs mixing with deep breaths, I thought about what to do. I decided to go back and check on him.

Crouching next to the young cop, I put my right palm over his nose and my left palm against his carotid artery. The right picked up a steady breath, while the left felt a fast but steady pulse. I felt the back of his head. There was no bleeding. I looked around me. The street was deserted. I thought about running away and then noticed the gun hanging from the cop's waist. With my luck, there were plenty of ways that this could end badly. Letting out a long, long sigh, I picked up the police cap off the ground and stood up.

I dragged the young cop's body to an empty space in the monthly parking lot nearby. I propped him up against the wall. I wheeled the bicycle to the lot, too. Since there was nothing else to do but wait for the cop to regain consciousness, I decided to have a smoke.

I sat on the pavement with my back against the wall and lit up a cigarette. I took a deep drag and exhaled deeply. I thought I heard birds chirping in the distance. Morning wasn't too far off.

When I finished my cigarette, the young cop woke up. He lay there for a while, his eyes darting here and there, and tried to get a grasp on the situation. We locked eyes a couple of times. I smiled at him.

I lit up another cigarette, and the cop sat up and felt around his body to see if anything was missing.

"I took out one bullet from your gun."

When I said this, the cop smiled at me grimly. He slid his body closer and sat next to me with his back against the wall.

"Give me one," said the young cop.

I gave him the whole pack. He pulled out a cigarette and stuck it in his mouth. I offered up the lighter and lit it. The cop brought his head closer and lit the end of his cigarette. He took a deep drag, exhaled, and said, "I'm not cut out for this job."

I looked at him, saying nothing.

The cop continued. "I graduated from a sports science university, you know? I ended up a policeman because I couldn't find a company that'd take me. Since this is kind of a default job, my heart's not in it. Look at what you did to me back there. I was a handball player. I'm no good at that martial arts stuff."

"That wouldn't have helped you," I said. "It's a close combat move used by the American military."

"Really?"

I nodded and said, "So you shouldn't get down on yourself."

The young cop gave a relieved smile and savored his cigarette.

For a while I listened to the cop complain about this and that. About being bullied by his senpai, about his slim prospects of getting promoted, about not being able to find a girlfriend, stuff like that. And before I knew it, I was telling him everything about what happened with Sakurai at the hotel. The cop listened to my story intently. After I finished, he said, "Wow, I would've done it first and thought about telling her later. You're a better man than I am." He said, "Good self-control." Then he said, "So which celebrity does she look like?"

When I thought about it and answered, "I don't know," the cop got all weird and said, "Come on, help a guy out here. You can't put the brakes on my imagination like that."

"She told me that I scared her," I said. "To be honest, I was devastated."

"I know what you're feeling." The cop lit up his fourth cigarette and said, looking far away, "A girl once told me that I was gross."

"That's harsh," I said.

"Just thinking about it is enough to make me want to cry, even now."

"It's best you forget about stuff like that," I said.

"Can *you* forget what happened tonight so easily?"

I shook my head.

"Right?" said the cop.

"I really liked her."

"So did I." The young cop blew smoke out of his nose. "Well, in my case I got rejected before we even started dating."

I lit another cigarette, took a deep drag, and said, "I didn't give a damn when someone discriminated against me. People that hate don't understand anything you try to tell them, so I just got used to hitting them. I wasn't ever going to lose a fight, so I was okay with it. Even if people like that continued to discriminate against me, I'd probably be okay with it."

I took another drag and exhaled.

"But ever since I met her, I've been scared as hell. It was the first time I felt that way. I guess I've never met a Japanese person that I really cared about before. In the first place, I didn't exactly know how to treat her, and what if I told her about my background and she hated me? Once I got to thinking about that, I couldn't bring myself to tell her. Even when I believed she wasn't the kind of girl to be prejudiced. But I guess in the end, I didn't trust her. Sometimes I wish my skin was green or something. That way, the good people will come closer and the haters will keep their distance. That would make things so much easier."

We both fell silent and each smoked a cigarette to ash.

Pulling out another cigarette, the young cop said, "I had this senpai three years my senior in university, a Zainichi guy named Kim-san, who everyone called Fearsome Kim. He had the fastest legs on the soccer team and was really strong. One time he beat the hell out of some racists on the karate team, and from then on, he was called Fearsome Kim. I watched that fight—it was incredible. There wasn't a single wasted motion in his movements. I guess it was what you'd call artistic. He didn't seem human. One guy took one of Kim's uppercuts in the chin and lifted off the ground. That image is burned in my memory even now. Ever since I saw that, I idolized him. How do I explain it—it had nothing to do with him being Zainichi. I just looked up to Kim-san."

The young cop nodded again and again, muttering, "He was something else," and lit his cigarette. I told the cop what I suspected might be Fearsome Kim's full name. The cop looked at me surprised and asked how I knew him. I explained to him that Fearsome Kim came to my junior high school as the new PE teacher during my second year and that he was feared by the students.

"I had a friend who was horrible at math. Probably couldn't recite the multiplication table, so he sure as hell wasn't going to follow the math lectures. One day he ditched the midwinter endurance run in PE class and was taking a nap in the classroom near the stove when Fearsome Kim appeared."

The young cop listened with rapt attention.

"Fearsome Kim walked right up, dragged the kid to his feet by the collar, and gave him a double slap in the face that nearly tore his head off. From that moment on, my friend was a wiz at math."

The young cop let out a disbelieving puff of smoke and said, "What?"

I said, "After those slaps in the face, he went to the hospital complaining of a terrible headache. They found out his brain waves were scrambled."

The young cop muttered, "Kim's slap will do that to you."

"The headaches went away after a week, and all of sudden, he could solve all those algebra and geometry problems he couldn't before. The same kid that used to say four times nine is twenty-eight."

"Are you serious?"

"It's true," I answered. "Not only was he able to solve junior-high-level problems, he could do high-school-level problems and came to be called the biggest genius since the school's founding. I heard he's working on proving Fermat's theorem in high school now."

"What is that—is it harder than quadratic equations?" asked the cop.

"The difference between Little League and the Major League."

The young cop nodded like he was impressed. "Sounds like your friend owes Kim-san big."

Really? For slapping him silly?

The cop said I should get going, put out his cigarette, and rose to his feet with his cap in hand. I stood up along with him. After patting me on the shoulder, the cop smiled a bit bashfully and said, "You should be like Fearsome Kim. Then you'd have all kinds of women hanging all over you."

I bowed my head and said, "I'm sorry about earlier."

The cop brought his mouth up to my ear and said, "Let's just keep that between us."

I nodded, laughing. The cop gave me an embarrassed smile.

When I returned home, my father was waiting up for me.

"What were you doing?" he asked.

I left out the part about Sakurai and told him about hanging out with a cop I'd hit. My father let out a deep sigh and muttered, "Whatever." Then he asked, "Are you all right?"

I nodded.

After a quick shower, I went back to my room. I stacked all the novels, poetry collections, art books, photography books, and CDs that Jeong-il had lent me in piles on my desk. Thirty-four books and sixteen CDs in all. I put Schubert's *Winter Journey*—one of Jeong-il's favorites—on low and began paging through all of Jeong-il's books.

Flipping through the pages of Langston Hughes's poetry collection, I noticed a sticky note on one of the pages for the first time. It was a page with a short poem called "Advice." I won't say any more about it. For as long as the poem remains unknown, it belongs only to me. No, it belongs only to me even if it does become known.

By the time I got done going through all the books, the sun had come up, and it was time to get ready for school. After some thought, I decided to skip school. As soon as I decided, I began to cry. Putting my forehead down on the desk, I cried for almost an hour. It was the first time I'd cried in a really long time.

I climbed under the covers and wished Jeong-il a good night before going to sleep.

Good night.

6

Sakurai hadn't called since the night of Jeong-il's funeral. I hadn't called her either.

And then one night about a week after the funeral, I got a call from Kato.

"It's been a while." Kato's voice lacked energy. "How've you been? Good?"

"Yeah, never mind that. Why haven't you been in school?"

Kato hadn't been in school for almost a month.

"So you haven't heard any rumors yet?"

"Did something happen?" I asked.

"I got pinched by the police."

"Doing what?"

"Selling acid."

"Dumb ass."

"Exactly."

"And?"

"I got sent to family court and somehow got off on probation. I've been seeing my probation officer every weekend, like we're dating or something. This dude is as cute as a button," he joked. "We're going to get engaged soon."

"Dumb ass."

"Exactly."

"What are you going to do now?"

"My old man was fuming that I got kicked out of school. I guess he thought I was a good kid. Anyway, I guess I'll live like a Zen monk and play it humble for a while."

"Okay. Enjoy your ascetic training."

"By the way, how's it going with your snow spirit?"

"She melted and disappeared."

"So you guys are finished?"

"You heard me."

"Oh. Have you decided about your future?"

"I'm applying to university."

"What's this all of a sudden?"

"A dying wish of a friend."

"What?"

"I'll tell you about it sometime. Anyway, I've been studying for the entrance exams."

"I'm sure you'll get in."

"You think?"

"Definitely. But if you're going to go through the trouble, you might as well get into a really good school. And then you can breathe the air up there for me."

"The air up there ain't nothing but thin and dirty."

"That's perfect. I mean, you're used to that."

We both let out a laugh.

"I'll come and see you soon," I said.

"Nah, better not," replied Kato.

"What's the matter?"

After a brief silence, Kato said, "I don't plan on seeing you for a while. As dumb as I am, I got to thinking after that incident at the club, and that's what I decided. I've been expecting too many people to carry me. I've been half-assed and pathetic. When I saw you going down the stairs to punch that kid, Kobayashi, I realized I'd never measure up to you. So until I can stand on my own two feet and get to where you are, I've decided that I'm not going to see you."

"I'm not the person you think I am."

"Look, maybe to you, you're just being normal. But not to me. I can't just be the yakuza's son anymore. It's not enough. It's not enough if I want to catch up to you. I have to look good and hard for my own thing. It isn't always easy being Japanese either." Kato chuckled sheepishly.

I said, "When I get into a really great university, I'll call you. Who knows how long that'll take."

"Hey, when that happens, I'll throw you a huge party."

"Say hi to your father for me."

"I'll tell him."

I said, "See you," and Kato said, "Later," and we each hung up the phone.

Around the start of November, a new challenger appeared before me. He was a second-year who'd mistakenly gotten it into his head that I'd become depressed without Kato around to back me. I put him away in a minute. That was a personal best. Thus, I was still undefeated with a 25–0 record. But just how long did I have to keep fighting like this anyway?

With Kato out of the picture, I didn't have anyone to talk to, so I concentrated on the entrance exams. I spent the breaks between classes and my lunch hour studying. When school ended, I went straight home and did my usual training routine and guitar practice and then studied until morning. Oh, and I picked up Spanish as a breather between studying for the exams. *Uno, dos, tres, cuatro, buenos días, muchas gracias, adiós, hasta la vista . . .*

My parents had another fight, and my mother left the house again. This time it was about my mother wanting to get a driver's license. Whatever.

There were a lot of rainy days. I focused on my studies, at times listening to the gloomy echo of raindrops.

On a rainy day toward the end of November, an unfamiliar face approached my desk during lunch hour. The voices in the gallery died down, and everyone around me moved off to the corners of the classroom. I closed the classics study guide I'd been reading and got into combat mode. The kid had a faint smile on his lips as if to show he came in peace.

"Can I talk to you for a minute?"

He had a soft voice. He was wearing silver-rimmed glasses. You had to be some kind of fighter if you were going to pick a fight with your glasses on. This kid didn't look like any kind of fighter.

I nodded, and the kid turned the chair from the desk in front of me around and sat down. The conversations in the gallery picked up again.

"My name is Miyamoto. You don't know me, do you?" he asked.

I answered honestly.

Miyamoto said, "That figures," and gave me a broad smile. "We've been in the same year for three years."

"What do you want?" I asked.

The smile vanished from Miyamoto's face. He casually looked around him and said in a flat voice, "I'm actually Zainichi, like you."

Miyamoto waited for some kind of response. A positive one, probably. I gave him nothing. A hint of disappointment came over his face.

"Unlike you, I've gone through the Japanese school system, so I don't know Korean or anything about Korean history or culture. But I'm still Korean. It's weird. Don't you think?"

I said nothing and stared at his face. Miyamoto continued, unbothered. "If I had been born in America, I'd be called Korean-American and would have all the rights accorded to an American citizen. I'd be treated like I was human. But this country is different. If I become a model person, more so than any Japanese, I still won't be treated like a proper human as long as I have Korean citizenship. The way a sumo wrestler can't become a stable master while he still has foreign citizenship. Assimilation or exclusion. There are only two choices in this country."

"Then why don't you change your citizenship to Japanese?" I said.

An obvious look of disappointment came over Miyamoto's face.

"Are you saying that I should admit defeat to this country?"

"What defeat? What are you fighting anyway? What—is your ethnic pride so fragile that it would disappear just by changing your citizenship?"

Miyamoto sighed and said, "Look, we don't have a lot of time left, so I'll tell you why I'm here. I'm trying to get all the young Zainichi together to form a group. We don't discriminate between North and South Korean or between Chongryon and Mindan. We already have close to a hundred members. I'm asking if you'd join our group. I know we'd be a lot stronger with someone like you on our side."

Miyamoto peered into my eyes as if to coax an answer out of me. As I sat there, saying nothing, he said, "Can I ask you something?"

I nodded.

"You have South Korean citizenship, right?"

I nodded again.

Miyamoto continued. "If you don't have any qualms about changing your citizenship, then why are you still South Korean?"

I didn't answer.

A faint smile flickering on the edges of his lips, Miyamoto said, "Please don't tell me it's because it doesn't affect the way you live. What about having to report to the government office every couple of years under the pretense of switching your alien registration? Or what about having to apply for a reentry permit before going overseas? We were born and raised here, and yet we have to ask permission to be allowed back in? Doesn't it all have a huge effect on the way someone like you lives?"

After a brief silence, I opened my mouth. "Who do you think you are? You don't know anything about me."

The bell chimed the end of lunch hour.

Miyamoto clicked his tongue and rose to his feet. "Just when it was getting interesting. I'll be back. You can give me an answer then."

I went home, thinking about everything Miyamoto said.

No one seemed to be there. My mother had entered her third week away from the house. I peeked into the living room and found a putter lying on the floor and golf balls scattered everywhere. I picked up the putter and leaned it against the sofa.

Night came and my father still hadn't come home. Just as I was thinking about what to order for dinner, my father called on the phone. He was really drunk.

"Hey, are you studying or what?"

"Have you been drinking?"

"Yep."

"That's not like you."

"I quit drinking the day you were born, so it's been eighteen years."

"What is it? Did something good happen?"

"The opposite."

"What happened?"

"I'll tell you about it later. Right now I need you to bring me some cash."

"Huh?"

"I ran out of money, and I can't pay the bill."

"You're killing me."

"Sorry."

I got an address and hung up the phone. I changed my clothes, took out the rest of the condolence money from the desk drawer, and put it in my pocket. I left the house, locking the door behind me. The rain, which had been coming down since morning, had finally let up.

My father stood slumped against the wall next to the main street exit of Ueno Station. He looked like he might slide down the wall and crumple on the ground any second. Next to him stood an unhappy-looking young man.

I went through the ticket barrier and up to my father. I patted his shoulder. His body twitched as he opened his eyes.

"Oh, my dutiful son," he said, a wide smile spreading across his face. His breath blew into my face, reeking of alcohol.

"Would you pay this man his money pl-eeze?"

My father pointed at the young man. I asked him how much and paid him.

"Maybe you should tell your father to carry a credit card," said the young man sarcastically.

Quite a few years back, my father applied for a credit card and was rejected on the background check. At the time, he had money to burn. The reason for the rejection was obvious: he was Korean. Ever since then, my father had a thing against credit cards.

Annoyed, I thought of pushing the guy around a little, but my father, perhaps sensing my irritation, pushed the young man's back and said to have a good night, as if to send him on his way. The young man clicked his tongue and moved off.

"Can you walk?" I asked.

"Sure I can," my father slurred as he walked off toward the ticket machines. He dragged his feet like an actor playing drunk in a comedy sketch. His pants were muddy around the waist. I fell in line next to him and held him by the waist.

"Let's get a taxi," I suggested.

My father put his arm around my shoulder and asked if I had enough money. I nodded. As I helped my father walk slowly toward the taxi stand, he muttered, "I took two phone calls back-to-back today . . .

the first one was that I was losing another one of my prize-exchange booths. The other was an international call from North Korea to tell me that Tong-il died."

I stopped walking. Tong-il was my uncle who had moved to North Korea.

"How did he die?" I asked.

"Some kind of illness. The call was from his wife. She said something about high blood pressure or malnutrition. I couldn't make out what she was trying to say so I'm not sure what the direct cause was. We were on the phone for about half an hour, and she spent about twenty-five minutes blaming me. About how I lived such a good life but never sent my younger brother anything."

"You sent him plenty," I said in a firm tone.

"Guess it wasn't enough."

My father urged me forward, saying, "Let's go." So I started walking again.

We got in a taxi and told the elderly driver the destination.

The taxi got caught in traffic and moved at a snail's pace. Maybe because it was the end of the month and a weekend night. For a while, my father and I were quiet, sitting buried in our seats. My father looked out the front windshield in a daze. Meanwhile, I thought about the uncle that I'd never meet. How long would it take to go from Japan to North Korea by plane? Two hours? Three? I could spend roughly the same number of hours and actually arrive in South Korea. But not North Korea. How did that come to be? In the first place, both Koreas are nothing more than pieces of land. What was prohibiting me from going to North Korea? The deep ocean? The tall mountains? The big sky? It was humans. The sons of bitches that put themselves there and roped off the territory as their own were the ones keeping me from seeing my uncle. Can you believe it? Everyone's always talking about how the technology boom has brought the world closer, but I still can't go to a place that's only hours away. I will never forgive the arrogant sons of bitches in North Korea. Ever.

The taxi cleared the traffic and began to cruise at a good speed.

"Tong-il was good at drawing," my father suddenly began. "Soon after the war, the family moved from Osaka to Okayama near a fishing port. We didn't stay very long, so I can't exactly remember where. Instead of school, I went to the port every day and did simple chores like unloading the cages filled with the day's catch from the fishing boats and cleaning the boats to get some food to eat for dinner. Since Aboji and Omoni found good work in Yamaguchi, I was in charge of looking after Tong-il. Every day Tong-il passed the time on the embankment drawing pictures with charcoal until I got done working. I was so worried that he might fall into the sea from the embankment. Tong-il could get so absorbed when he was drawing. One day, the port union boss took a look at Tong-il's drawings and had Tong-il paint a picture on the bow of his fishing boat. It was a picture of a sun rising up over the sea. It was well drawn, and the union boss seemed happy with it. Three days later, the boss's boat encountered a storm at sea. When it got dark, and the boat still hadn't returned, everyone gave the boat and crew up for lost, but then the boat returned the next morning. Since that incident, rumor spread that Tong-il's picture was a good luck charm, and suddenly people wanted Tong-il to paint something on *their* boats. Fishermen can be a superstitious lot. Tong-il quickly became a popular painter, and soon he was the one looking after me. Once he brought home a whole crab, something even I hadn't done. I was so proud of him. That was the first time I ever ate crab. Tong-il, too. As embarrassing as this may sound, we cried while we ate, saying again and again how good it tasted. I wonder if he ever ate crab up north. Maybe I should have sent him some crab."

It was a good story. My father's eyes had welled up with tears. I guess the ideal scenario would have been for me to put my arm around him and say cheer up, and for my father to become overcome with emotion and hug me. Not a chance. This old man has worked me over my entire life.

In the spring of my second year in junior high school, I stole a moped and got caught, naturally without a license, and with two others riding with me to boot. Because I'd been caught doing all sorts of bad things in the past, this time it was entirely possible that I wouldn't get off with a misdemeanor but would be sent to family court.

My father came down to the station and said, "I'm sorry for what my son has done," and pleaded for a misdemeanor charge. The instant he saw me, the old man drilled a hard right hook to my temple. Already half unconscious, I was hit in the liver with a left body hook, which was quickly followed by another left hook in the face.

In boxing this was called a double left hook. Because of the body hook, I started vomiting; because of the left hook, I broke a molar. The tooth came out of my mouth along with stomach fluid. My father grabbed me as I was vomiting on the floor, pulled me up by the collar, and landed a right straight squarely on my chin. I don't exactly remember what happened after that. Only the voice of the interrogating detective screaming, "Please forgive him! He's going to die!" was echoing inside my head. When I came to, I was lying in the back seat of my father's car. Somehow I managed to sit up and found my father beaming at me in the rearview mirror.

"You got off with no strikes on your record," he said, chuckling. "Be grateful."

That's when I swore to myself: someday I'm going to kill this son of a bitch with my own hands.

Anyway, so much for the ideal scenario for my father and me. Besides, until *I* gave my father the sound beating he deserved, he wasn't going to be brought to his knees by anything—no matter what. Regardless of whether his business was taken away by the state, or whether his beloved younger brother died, he wasn't going to show weakness. The only thing that was going to knock this man down—a man who'd never gone down in a fight ever—was me.

And so I said, "Will you stop with the crab? Geez, you sound pathetic. The days when people are going to cry over your sorry sob story are over. It's because you first- and second-generation Zainichi are so piss-poor that my generation can't shine."

With tears still in his eyes, my father looked at me, shocked. I continued. "If the people up north want to eat crab, then start a freakin' revolution. What the hell are they doing up there?"

The tears began to recede from my father's eyes.

I said, "Your brother must have resented you. While he was struggling, you were off in Hawaii playing golf. I bet he's going to show up at your pillow tonight as a ghost. *Aloha!*"

A stench of alcohol so thick you could grab it came wafting from my father's entire body. His pores must have opened. His face was a different shade of red than before. I decided to finish him off.

"You know what? Your days are over. Your sad, pathetic days are finished."

An aura of alcohol and murder emanated from my father's body. As he opened his mouth to say something, the taxi, which had been cruising along, suddenly screeched its brakes and stopped on the side of the road. After putting the car in park, the elderly taxi driver turned around. His face was crimson.

"How dare you talk to your father like that!" he shouted at me.

I guess I was universally incompatible with taxi drivers.

My father said, "Looks like you got touched in the head from all that studying."

I answered, "Shut up, you punch-drunk."

My father took a deep breath and said to the taxi driver, "Please wait here. We're going to settle this outside."

My father and I got out of the taxi and scanned the area. There was a park entrance up at the other end of the sidewalk. Silently we started walking that way. The taxi driver followed behind us.

The park was big. The circular space where we entered was surrounded by benches. On the benches sat several young couples, flirting with each other. My father and I went to the center of the circle and faced each other about two yards apart. A halogen light shined like a spotlight on both of us. The taxi driver stood a bit off center between us, like a referee. For an instant, my mother's face came to mind.

My mother would say to me, "If you ever lay a hand on your father, I'm going to kill you and then kill myself."

It was the last sentiment of Confucian spirit my mother still had inside her. But no way was I going to back down now. No matter what.

I steeled myself. I took a breath so my father wouldn't notice and held it in my belly.

My father opened his mouth and said in a mocking tone, "Come, Luke."

Shut up.

After bending my knees into a near squat, I kicked off from the balls of my feet and dove inside his reach. Although the human eye can easily pick up lateral movements, it's difficult to react to vertical movements. The average person would panic at the sight of me attacking from below and be KO'd with one punch, defenseless. But my father, a former nationally ranked boxer, was different. He instinctively brought his arms together in front of his face like a shield. In a split second, I changed my line of attack from the face to my father's body. My left hook landed squarely on his liver. The average person would reflexively lower his guard to protect his body and take a second left hook in the face. My father didn't lower his guard. I tested him again and delivered a right hook to his ribs. He let out a groan but kept his arms hard against his face.

Around the time my father first started teaching me to box, he often would say this: "Don't let yourself get knocked down by a body blow. You'll never be an elite boxer. You've got to harden up the body. Take as many punches in the body as you can and sap your opponent of his power. But make sure you guard your head. Even if your body gets beat up, as long as you have your head, you have a chance. Always."

I kept pounding him in the body so as not to give him an opening to counterattack. But God, he was hard. Really hard. It was hard to believe this was the body of a man who would turn sixty in a couple of years. Who the hell did he think he was? What did you have to eat to get a body like this?

I was getting impatient. I sidestepped his guard and began punching the side of his face. Aiming for the part right under the ear, I unleashed a steady series of hooks right and left. A good hit there could numb the semicircular canal, causing the opponent to lose his sense of balance, making it easier to knock him down. I got a couple of good hits in, and my father's knees gradually grew wobbly. His arms, which were held up against his face, slowly began to separate to the sides to protect his ears. If I kept attacking below the ears, his arms would separate even more, leaving his face wide open, and I'd be able to punch him in the nose. Then I'd win. I'd make my father's knees touch the mat for the first time.

I continued to pound him with my hook, silently willing his arms to open. Open! His arms split apart about four inches, and I sighted my father's nose and mouth. His nose was where it usually was. But his lips. He had curled his lower lip inside his mouth and was biting down on it with his front teeth. He didn't seem to be doing it to bear the pain. Suddenly his mouth started making a *chuuu chuuu* sound, like he was sucking something. The old man was biting his lip and sucking something at the same time. When I got wise to his trick, it was too late.

Suddenly my father let down his guard. The instant his eyes shone, reflecting the halogen light, the blood came spraying out of his mouth. Because I'd been mesmerized by the light in his eyes, I closed my eyes too late. A fight is always decided in an instant. The blood flew into my eyes and blinded me.

I took three punches to the face. Boom. Boom. Boom. The first punch hit me like a hunk of concrete and made my spine creak. I felt the second punch break one of my front teeth. I locked my guard in front of my face. I took a heavy punch in the ribs, right and left. I let down my guard. Then a hook under the left ear. For an instant, a pale flame floated up and disappeared before my closed eyes. In the next instant, I collapsed. I lay down, putting my back flat on the ground. The earth was teetering unsteadily. I was going to be sick. Someone, stop the earth from tilting. My father's voice came down from above. The earth stopped.

"What idiot lets down his guard?"

After spitting out the blood pooled in my mouth, somehow I managed to squeeze out the words, "That . . . was . . . dirty."

My father's stern voice pelted my body. "Sorry. But this is how *we've* managed to scrap out a win. I can't change my ways now."

I rubbed my eyes to try to see in the direction of the voice. But I couldn't quite wipe the blood—my father's blood—out of my eyes. Still I looked in the direction the voice was coming from. Maybe it was because I was looking up at him, but my father looked huge in my eyes. The taxi driver went to him, grabbed his right arm, and raised it above his head. The bystanders around us broke into applause. There were even a few whistles. Amid congratulations from the taxi driver and the couples, my father smiled, embarrassed. My eyes hurt, so I closed them. The tears came naturally. Blinking several times, I squeezed out the blood mixed with tears from my eyes. The applause and cheers did not stop.

Damn it, damn it, damn it . . .

◆ ◆ ◆

After I washed off the blood at the water fountain, I got in the taxi again.

I stared at the broken tooth in the palm of my hand. As I was cleaning off my face at the fountain, the taxi driver had come and given it to me. I traced what was left of my front tooth with my tongue. A pain shot through my head every time I breathed through my mouth. Maybe the nerve was exposed. I opened the window halfway and tossed the broken tooth outside. My father muttered, "You may be right about something."

"About what?" I asked.

"That my generation's time has passed."

I looked at my father's profile. The bruise on his chin was beginning to turn from red to blue. There were teeth marks etched clearly on his lower lip dotted with lots of tiny scab-spots.

"This country is gradually beginning to change. And will continue to change. Zainichi or Japanese—pretty soon that's not going to matter anymore. That's why your generation should set your sights outward."

"Really?" I asked in earnest. "Do you really think this country will change?"

Whatever his reasoning might've been, he gave me a sure nod. A confident smile was spread across his face. Reasoning? There wasn't any reasoning required. What was important was to believe. Definitely.

"Is everything going to be okay at work?"

"Yeah," he said spiritedly. "I still have one booth. I never planned to stay in this business for very long or have you take it over, so if I finish with zero in the end, I'll be all right with that. Your mother and I already have enough saved up to enjoy retirement. But you're on your own."

My father let out a hearty laugh. He never got past elementary school, yet taught himself to read Marx and Nietzsche. With his concrete body and a mind as sharp as ice, he's continued to fight and survive in this tough country. Deep down, I knew why this bastard had suddenly changed his citizenship to South Korean. He didn't do it so he could go to Hawaii. He did it for me. He was trying to unburden me from one of the shackles chained to my legs. I knew why this beautiful bastard had decorated the foyer with that embarrassing picture of him being kissed on the cheek as he was flashing a peace sign. It was because he knew that by turning his back on Chongryon and Mindan, he would lose most of his friends and acquaintances. No one in this country was going to give this crazy old guy his due for continuing to fight all on his own. That's why I decided to tell him.

"I'll erase these national borders someday."

After staring at me in amazement at these words, my father flashed an invincible smile and said, "You should know our family hails from a long line of bullshit artists dating back to the Joseon Dynasty."

My father and I looked at each other and laughed. The taxi stopped at a light back near our neighborhood. From outside the rolled-down window of the taxi came the unseasonal sound of a summer wind-bell in the distance.

Chirr-rin chirr-rin, chirr-rin chirr-rin . . .

My father let slip a cherubic smile and said, "The sound brings back memories." I didn't know whether there was a custom of hanging wind-bells in Korea. I'm pretty sure my father didn't know either.

We arrived in front of our house. The taxi driver refused to take my father's money.

"You've shown me something far more special. Please use the money to send your brother some flowers."

The light was on in the house. This wasn't good. I steeled myself and went inside. My mother came to the door and took one look at us, and her face changed color in an instant. She ran past my father and me and disappeared out the door. Ten seconds later, she came back with a bamboo broom in her hands. She beat me with the butt end of the broom thirty-eight times. My father stood there, watching, and said, "Now that'll teach you the power of love," and let out a belly laugh. My mother beat him three times.

I became so bruised and feverish that I stayed home from school for three days.

Lunch break.

An uncomfortable air filled the classroom.

When I'd opened my mouth and answered the teacher's question during second-period Japanese class, everyone found out my front tooth was chipped. Challengers were likely to come gunning for me today.

The classroom door rattled open. Everyone's eyes flew in that direction. With a disappointed sigh, they went back to talking to their friends.

Miyamoto turned the chair around and sat down in front of me, like before.

"So did you give it some thought?" he asked.

"You can keep me out of it," I answered.

Miyamoto let out a short sigh and said, "If you don't mind, would you at least tell me why? So I can take notes for next time."

After I thought about it, I answered, "It's got nothing to do with what you're trying to do. I think it's right, and it's important. I'm trying to accomplish the same thing but in my own way."

Miyamoto smiled cynically. "I figured you for a realist."

I let out a scornful laugh. "I *am* a realist. I've got my eye on something different, that's all."

Miyamoto, with the same cynical smile on his face, said, "Go ahead. Try to do it on your own, if you can. Careful that this country doesn't squash you first."

I stared quietly at Miyamoto's face for a while, then said, "Look, I don't have any beef with you. Like I said, what you're trying to do is right. I just can't be a part of it, that's all. I'm busy."

The look of cynicism vanished from Miyamoto's face. "Busy? With what?"

"There's someone I have to beat. To beat him, I need to study and get myself stronger. There isn't any going forward until I defeat him. But when I do, I'll be all but invincible. I can even change the world."

My fight record since I started high school now sat at 25–1. I was no longer the undefeated king. That one loss was a huge one.

Miyamoto shook his head like he had no clue what I was talking about.

I said, "The reason I don't change my nationality is because I don't want to be incorporated or assimilated or strapped down by any country. I'm tired of living feeling like I'm a part of some big system. And that includes your little group."

Miyamoto opened his mouth to say something, but I cut him off. "But if Kim Basinger ever asked me to change my nationality, I'd go down and fill out the forms right now. That's all that nationality is to me. But maybe that just makes me a hypocrite."

Miyamoto, who'd been staring at me with a stern look and his mouth half open, loosened up and smiled. "Now if you're talking Catherine Deneuve . . ."

"What are you, a hundred?"

"Shut up."

We gave each other a look and laughed—just as the door at the front of the classroom flew open.

I told Miyamoto, "You should get out of the way."

Miyamoto got up from the chair and stuck his hand out at me. We exchanged a firm handshake.

I shifted my gaze from Miyamoto retreating to safety in the corner to the challenger coming at me. I thought about what one-liner I should go with today. Maybe that thing my father said would do the trick: *No soy coreano, ni japonés, soy un nómada desarraigado.*

I'm not Korean or Japanese. I'm a rootless vagabond.

Yeah, that's what I'll say.

7

The gloomy rainy days of November gave way to December.

I continued to put in some serious time studying for the entrance exams, while my mother put in some serious time at the driving school, and my father put in some serious time on the golf course.

One Sunday in the beginning of December, I went to Jeong-il's house to return all the stuff he'd lent me.

"I wish you'd hold on to them for Jeong-il," his mother said, smiling. "What happened to your tooth?"

She said that after some soul searching, she'd decided to scatter Jeong-il's ashes in different countries. "I'm planning to go to South Korea for the first time, soon."

When I offered to tag along as her interpreter, she said, "I'm desperately trying to learn Korean right now," and laughed cheerfully. "Such fun learning a language I don't know. I should have started sooner, when he was still alive . . ."

When I was ready to leave, Jeong-il's mother walked me to the door and said, "Please keep Jeong-il in your memories."

I answered, "Yes. Always."

◆　◆　◆

Sometime in the middle of December, my mother told me Naomi-san was getting married. The guy was an American businessman working at a foreign company, who came around the restaurant a lot. Taking a break between cram sessions, I went to the restaurant to congratulate her. When I did, Naomi-san smiled happily and said, "It's like the descendants of the two groups that went their own way somewhere in the Middle East all those years ago found each other in Japan. Isn't it wonderful?"

I nodded emphatically.

"Your chipped tooth is very cute," she said, giving my cheek a gentle stroke. "You have to get *cuter* and *get* yourself a nice girl and be *happier* than everyone else, all right?"

I nodded and teased, "You're using more English in your speech, Naomi-san."

For some reason Naomi-san's cheeks became flushed as she gave me a seductive smile.

On the evening of December 23, I accidentally bumped into Won-soo on the train platform at Ikebukuro Station.

I was on the Yamanote Line platform on my way to cram school, while Won-soo stood on the Saikyo Line platform on the opposite side. We spotted each other almost at the same time. He was there with three of his buddies. They noticed me, too. For a while we stood facing each other with the four rails sandwiched between us. Then a train pulled into Won-soo's side of the platform first, blocking them from view. Then a train pulled into my side of the platform soon after. I didn't get on the train. The trains departed, clearing my view. Won-soo and his buddies were gone. I moved to the middle of the platform where there was more room and waited. My fight record against Won-soo was 3–2, so I was one up on him.

After about a minute, Won-soo appeared. None of his buddies were with him. I stood where I was and waited for Won-soo to approach me. He stopped opposite me. He cast a piercing look, a deep line creasing his brow. It was a look I'd seen a million times. He wasn't the least bit intimidating. I couldn't help but flash a smile. A bemused expression came over his face for an instant at the sight of my tooth, but the severe look returned.

"Who did that to you?"

That was Won-soo. Anytime one of his own got hurt or disrespected, he didn't think twice. He was the first one out for revenge.

"It was my old man."

When I said this, his grim look faded. I flashed another smile at Won-soo, and he smiled a bit bashfully.

Won-soo stepped to the side so we were standing shoulder-to-shoulder. We now faced the platform where Won-soo had been only moments ago. After another train came and went, Won-soo, keeping his eyes trained straight ahead, said, "Do you remember the time we stole that moped and got caught riding it three deep?"

I kept looking straight ahead and nodded.

Won-soo said, "I'll never forget the way your *aboji* came into the police station and beat the living daylights out of you. I was so freaked he was going to beat me next that I thought about playing dead."

"What do you think, my old man's a bear?"

"Not any ordinary bear. A grizzly."

We laughed, our eyes still looking straight ahead.

Won-soo muttered, "Your aboji is cool . . ."

Won-soo's father had a habit of saying, "If I were born Japanese, I would've been prime minister or president of a company." Whenever he had a bad day at the factory, he got drunk and hit Won-soo. Won-soo had burn scars on his left shoulder blade, the right side of his belly button, right butt cheek, left thigh, and the top of his right foot, where his aboji had pressed a lit mosquito coil into him.

Won-soo ended up running away from home five times, and I went along with him every time. The first time was in the third grade when we got on the Tokaido line from Tokyo Station and went to Chigasaki. The next time we ran away to Odawara, then Atami, and Shizuoka after that, running farther away every time until finally we reached Nagoya and became pachinko kings. Running away was fun. Which made having to go back home and parting ways all the more difficult, and we resorted to trash talking each other about how the other had stupid-looking eyebrows or how one couldn't stand the way the other ate with his chopsticks or some such nonsense and got into a knock-down fight. Thus my 3–2 record against him. We went our separate ways, vowing never to go anywhere with each other again, and we were back to hanging out the next day like nothing had ever happened. I adored Won-soo.

Two trains came and went.

Won-soo spoke. "You said at the funeral that I never talked to Jeong-il. You're wrong about that. Actually, I did talk to him. We never talked about anything serious like you guys did. He talked about you a lot."

I turned toward him. He was still looking straight ahead. I looked forward again. Two more trains came and went. Countless passengers went past us. Won-soo and I stood absolutely still on the platform.

Won-soo said, "Look, I know what's up. I know that the North and Chongryon are only thinking about using us and can't be counted on. But I plan on making a go here on the inside. Believe it or not, I do have some guys depending on me. So long as I can fight for them, I won't have to be a screwup."

"Yeah, I know.

Two more trains.

Won-soo asked, "What do you talk about in that Japanese school of yours?"

"I don't really talk to anyone."

"Do you have any friends?"

"Nah."

"Oh . . ."

Two more trains.

Won-soo said, "If we live long enough to become tired old geezers, we should go to the hot springs together."

"Nah, farther than that. We should go to Hawaii."

"Hawaii . . . that sounds great."

Two more trains.

Won-soo said, "That day you did the Test of Courage? You were pretty cool."

"Yeah."

Another train.

Won-soo said, "Go, get on the train already."

"Yeah."

Another train.

Won-soo said, "*Go*. I let you off today for that hit at the funeral."

"Shut up. I'll go when I want."

Another train.

Won-soo said, "Go, unless you want to get decked. I can't stand the way you live your life."

I felt his eyes on me. I turned toward him. Won-soo was looking at me, smiling like he was about to cry.

Tell me, Won-soo. What does my face look like now? I can't tell . . .

Another train was coming. After taking a step forward, I managed to squeeze out the words, "Don't get yourself killed."

Still smiling back his tears, Won-soo jerked his chin up defiantly, the same chin that must've repelled dozens of my punches, and said, "They're not going to kill me so easily."

The train slid into the platform and came to a stop. I casually raised a hand and said, "See ya," and walked forward. I felt Won-soo's old, familiar gaze on my back. I boarded the train. Even after the doors shut behind me, I could still feel his gaze on me. I didn't turn around until the train had completely pulled out of the station.

Christmas Eve.

I'd been holed up in my room, studying for the entrance exams since morning, when my father poked his head in and gave a sinister laugh.

"Quiet."

After he closed the door, I could hear him singing.

The old man must've learned lyrics to that Tatsuro Yamashita song about spending Christmas Eve alone just so he could throw dirt in my face. Jackass.

At night, the phone rang. My father shouted, "Phone!" from below. My father and mother never answered the phone when they were playing chess. Reluctantly I put down my pencil and picked up the cordless in my room. It was Sakurai.

"I haven't seen you for ages," she said.

I hesitated.

"How have you been?" she asked.

I kept quiet.

Sakurai continued anyway. "I'm doing great."

After a brief silence, Sakurai seemed to finally work up the courage. "You remember the elementary school, don't you? Can you meet me there now? I'll wait for you."

She hung up the phone. I switched off the phone and lay down on the bed. I thought about this and that for about five minutes, but my decision was obvious from the start. I got up and started to change. I put on a white long-sleeved shirt and jeans and got into a black down jacket. I took out what little was left of the condolence money from the desk drawer and stuffed it into my jeans pocket.

"I'm going out for a while."

My mother and father looked up from the chess pieces on the board at the same time.

My mother said, "Didn't I tell you to cap that tooth?"

Telling my mother to be quiet, I went out into the foyer. As I put on my shoes, I could hear my father doing his best rendition of Bing Crosby.

> Silent night, holy night
> All is calm, all is bright

I thought you were a Marxist, for Christ's sake.
I left the house.

It took me an hour and a half to arrive in front of the iron gate of the elementary school.

I jumped over the gate and went inside the grounds. I looked around the schoolyard. Sakurai's white figure sitting on the bench next to the bronze bust of some famous person stood out in the darkness. Slowly I walked toward her. She was wearing a white duffle coat over a blue turtleneck sweater. She looked great. Her hair, which had grown, was parted on the left and pulled back behind her ears. Her intelligent forehead was showing. I adored Sakurai's forehead.

I stopped and stood in front of Sakurai. Her face was clouded with nervousness. I looked down at her, saying nothing. She smiled awkwardly and said, "Thanks for coming."

I kept silent.

"I've been looking up at the sky, waiting for you. Every time the moon disappeared behind the clouds, I was worried that it might start snowing. The forecast said that it was supposed to rain or snow today. Snow on Christmas Eve—isn't that just horrible? Meeting a boy like this on a snowy Christmas Eve . . . I'd just die of embarrassment. Unless of course I don't die from the cold first."

Sakurai let out a big sigh. Her white breath floated up and disappeared. The smile vanished from her face, and she said, "I've been thinking about a lot of things since we stopped seeing each other. And I've read a lot of books, a lot of difficult books and—"

I squatted down in front of her. It must have been sudden, as a tiny gasp escaped Sakurai's mouth. Her face was rigid with nerves. Looking up and giving her a hard look, I said, "Who am I?"

"What?"

"Who am I?"

After thinking about it for a moment, Sakurai answered, "You're Zainichi."

I turned around and after giving the pedestal of the bronze statue three good kicks, I faced Sakurai again and said, "I swear sometimes I want to just kill all you Japanese! How can you call us Zainichi without so much as a second thought? We were *born* in this country and *raised* in this country! Don't call us that like we're the same as the American military or Iranians that just stepped off the boat yesterday. Calling us Zainichi is the same as saying we're foreigners who'll eventually leave the country. Do you get that? Have you ever taken the time to think about that, even once?"

Sakurai swallowed and kept looking at me. I knelt down before her. "Who cares? If you people want to call me Zainichi, go ahead! You Japanese are scared of me. Can't feel safe unless you categorize and label it, right? But you're wrong. You know what—I'm a lion. A lion has no idea he's a lion. It's just a random name that you people gave him so you can feel like you know all about him. See what happens when you try to get closer, calling my name. I'll pounce on your carotid artery and tear you to shreds. You understand? As long as you call me Zainichi, you're always going to be my victim. I'm not Zainichi or South Korean or North Korean or Mongoloid. Quit forcing me into those narrow categories. I'm me! Wait, I don't even want to be me anymore. I want to be free from having to be me. I'll go anywhere to find whatever thing will let me forget who I am. And if that thing isn't here, I'll get out of this country, which is what you wanted anyway. You can't do that, can you? No, you'll all die, tied down by your ideas about country, land, titles, customs, tradition, and culture. Well, that's too bad. I never had any of that stuff, so I'm free to go anywhere I please. Jealous? Say you're jealous! Damn it, what am I saying? Damn it, damn it . . ."

Sakurai's hands reached out and found my cheeks. Her hands felt warm.

"Those eyes . . . ," she said, her voice trembling as she smiled faintly.

"Eyes?"

She nodded, smiling some more, and continued. "Last September, I got a horrible grade on my mock exams, and even though I knew how stupid it was to get all depressed about it, I was feeling depressed anyway. It was a rainy day after school, and I was thinking how I didn't want to go home just yet when I went by the gym, and there was a basketball game going on. I don't know anything about basketball, and I'm not the least bit interested, but for some reason, on that day I was drawn to the sound of the basketball hitting the court, so I just wandered in. At first I was kind of watching the game, but soon I couldn't take my eyes off one of the boys in the game. His movements were so graceful, like he was performing a choreographed dance. I just kept watching him, wishing that I could move like that. Suddenly the boy threw the basketball at the face of the boy guarding him. The other boy must've given him a nasty foul or said something terrible to him. It happened so suddenly, I was in shock. The court went quiet for a second, and then one kid on the same team as the boy who'd been hit charged the boy who threw the basketball. Then the boy jumped up in the air really high and drop-kicked the kid charging at him. I'd only seen pro wrestlers on TV drop-kick anyone, so I got really excited seeing it live. And if that wasn't enough, the boy dropped-kicked every one of the boys charging

158

him, one after the next. The time he was in the air must've been longer than the time on solid ground. I was so mesmerized by this boy's movements. The way he moved was so incredible. It was as if gravity didn't exist around him, at all. Like he'd changed the laws of nature. And just like that, all the players on the opposing team were on the floor with their noses bleeding and stuff. The refs finally came over to try to restrain the boy, but he was so worked up that he started drop-kicking the refs! By this point, everything was so ridiculous that I was laughing and laughing. Then the boy's coach turned to the players on the bench and said, 'Somebody stop Sugihara! Go!' In my heart I was screaming for you to run away, but it was no use. The moment you landed after drop-kicking a second ref, your teammates grabbed you. But you still fought back, shouting 'Let me go! Let me go!' Your teammates seemed reluctant, but after they managed to get you on the ground somehow, they piled on top of you. There were about four of them, I think, making like this mound on top of you. I was so devastated you'd been caught that I was stupidly almost in tears. But the tears stopped right away. The mound was heaving up and down. Up and down, even with four people piled on top of you. I just lost it and burst out laughing, rolling on the seats until my sides hurt. I was laughing so hard that that the tears started coming again.

"When I finally got ahold of myself and looked down, some of your senpai were smacking you across the face, and then your coach grabbed you by the back of the uniform and dragged you off the court to the locker room. It was hilarious. I mean, you looked like a naughty kitten being picked up by the scruff of the neck, about to be tossed outside. You and the coach walked over toward where I was sitting. I leaned out of my seat to follow you with my eyes. That's when you glared at me with these really intense eyes. I had you all wrong. You weren't a kitten, but a lion. And when you glared at me, I got shivers up and down my spine and felt weird inside, and then I realized I was wet . . . It was the first time that happened to me. I never got that way when I was kissed or touched by a boy before, but just you glaring at me got me wet. For a long time, I waited for you outside the school, but I guess you left from the back, so I couldn't meet you then. From that day, I had your name and the name of your high school stamped in my brain.

"A couple of times I thought about going to your high school, but I couldn't work up the courage because I'd never done something like that before. And when I talked to my friends about it, they warned me, saying, 'Don't get involved with anyone that goes to that stupid school.' And they even said, 'You'll get raped if you go anywhere near that school.' So in the end I couldn't bring myself to go.

"But I always knew that I was going to meet you someday. I was sure of it. So in April when a boy who sits next to me in class showed me the ticket to a party he'd been forced to buy, and I saw the party was being organized by someone from your school and heard that lots of boys from the school were going to be there, I asked for the boy's ticket because I knew I had to go. And when I went to the party, there you were, just like I'd known you'd be. I recognized you right away. Because you glared at me then, too. And then I got wet again."

Cupping my cheeks, Sakurai's hands seemed to tense. "I'm really excited right now. Do you want to feel?"

"Here?" I said, a bit off guard.

Sakurai nodded.

I wavered for a moment and answered, "Maybe this isn't the place . . ."

Suddenly Sakurai drew my face into her chest. With her hands on the back of my head and neck, she held me tight. *Ba-dump ba-dump.* I could hear the sound of her heart beating. That familiar sound. That comforting sound.

Sakurai's voice came from above. "I don't care what you are, Sugihara. As long as you jump for me and look at me with those eyes once in a while, I don't care if you don't speak Japanese. There isn't any-one, anywhere, who can jump and look at me like you do."

"Really?" I asked, my face still buried in her chest.

"Yes. I know that now. Actually, I might have known it since the first time I saw you."

Sakurai kissed the top of my head three times. Her arms relaxed around me, so I slowly raised my head from her chest. Sakurai looked at me and said, "Why are you crying?"

"No way," I said. "I can't cry when other people are around."

Sakurai narrowed her eyes as though she were looking at something bright, put her palms against my cheeks again, and wiped the tears on my face with her thumbs.

"I've been dying to tell you," she said, putting on a serious face. "That chipped tooth makes you look adorable."

We looked at each other and laughed. Letting go of my face, Sakurai stood up.

"The moon's about to hide behind the clouds again. Let's go somewhere before it begins to snow and ruins everything."

"Where do you want to go?"

"Anywhere. Somewhere warm first. We can think about where we're going to stay tonight."

"Are you sure?"

"Let's work on not asking such tiresome questions."

Sakurai moved past me and began skipping toward the main gate. Still kneeling on the ground, I chased after her with my eyes. Sakurai stopped and turned around. The most beautiful smile I'd ever seen spread across her face. Out of her mouth came a breath as white as snow and a warm voice: "Let's go."

ABOUT THE AUTHOR

Kazuki Kaneshiro graduated from Keio University and made his literary debut with *Revolution No. 3* in 1998, winning the Shosetsu Gendai Prize for New Writers. In 2000, Kaneshiro won the Naoki Prize for *GO*, which tackles issues of ethnicity and discrimination in Japanese society. The novel's film adaptation went on to win every major award in Japan in 2002. Many of his works have been made into films or manga, and Kaneshiro has been adept at working synergistically across multiple formats and genres, writing the original concepts and scripts for the TV series *SP* and *CRISIS*.

ABOUT THE TRANSLATOR

Takami Nieda was born in New York City and has degrees in English from Stanford University and Georgetown University. She has translated and edited more than twenty works of fiction and nonfiction from Japanese into English and has received numerous grants in support of her translations. Her translations have also appeared in *Words Without Borders*, *Asymptote*, and *PEN America*. Nieda teaches writing and literature at Seattle Central College in Washington State. She would like to acknowledge the PEN/Heim Translation Fund and the Japanese Literature Publishing and Promotion Center; this translation would not have been possible without their generous support.